Amy Peppercorn
Starry-Eyed and Screaming

John Brindley lives with his partner in the southeast of England. He has two children, both of whom have been instrumental in the development of his early stories for young people. John is a keen music fan and enjoys playing squash and socialising in London.

Amy Peppercorn
Starry-eyed and
Screaming

John Brindley

Dolphin Paperbacks

First published in Great Britain in 2003
as a Dolphin paperback
by Orion Children's Books
a division of the Orion Publishing Group Ltd
Orion House
5 Upper St Martin's Lane
London WC2H 9EA

A catalogue record for this book
is available from the British Library

Typeset at The Spartan Press Ltd,
Lymington, Hants

Printed in Great Britain by
Clays Ltd, St Ives plc

ISBN 1 84255 241 4

*** One

My name *is* Amy, by the way. My full name? As if you didn't know. It's Amy Peppercorn, no middle name. Amy Peppercorn, and I'm not kidding. That really is my name. I sound like something out of my twin sisters' little storybooks, don't I?

I hate my name. I've never met anybody with a name I've disliked more than my own. My best friend's called Rebecca Bradley. She says she doesn't like *her* name, but goes around calling herself Beccs Bradley, which sounds really good. Her cousin's called Kirsty McCloud, which has got an American accent, I don't know why; and it manages to sound dreamy.

But Amy Peppercorn? What can you do with it? My baby sisters are called Georgina and Joanna Peppercorn. We sound like such a bunch of – bunch of Peppercorns, don't we?

Anyway, the best place to start telling you about it is the evening after school when Beccs and me decided to go and wind up the boys in the band, if you could call it a band.

'Where we going?' Kirsten wanted to know, tagging on behind Beccs, like she always did, with her long legs and hair and no real mates of her own.

'We're going to see The Worst Band In The World,' I said, over my shoulder.

'Oh, good,' Kirsty said. 'I like them.'

Beccs laughed. I shook my head. Kirsty didn't know what she'd said. 'We're going to the school hall to watch The

1

Grunge Machine,' I said. 'They're the worst band in the world, with the worst band name, and you like them?'

Beccs laughed again, nervously.

Kirsty gave a little tight-lipped smile. 'Joke,' she said.

Beccs laughed. I didn't. Kirsty was always saying stupid things without meaning to, then claiming she was only joking. Beccs always tried to laugh; she is Kirsten's first cousin. I'm not. Not first, second; not any number. I'm not related to her in any way. I didn't have to laugh, just because Kirsten said it was a joke when I knew it wasn't.

'Come on,' Becca said, because we'd all stopped in the corridor. 'Let's go and enjoy the worst band in the world messing up the worst music in the world.'

If The Grunge Machine hadn't been so bad, maybe we wouldn't have got involved; if they could have put two notes together without making it feel as though your teeth were being filed down. They had a couple of old amps, lead guitar, drums and keyboards. They were supposed to be an indie band, except that indie isn't really supposed to make your ears bleed.

'What was that s'posed to be?' Peter Stevens was shouting at Michael Bradshaw.

'What we supposed to be playing?' Bradshaw stammered. 'I don't know what we're supposed to be playing.'

Long Geoffrey Fryer was peering down over the little shelf of his keyboards. 'You're s-s-singing the wrong l-lyrics,' he was trying to shout at Peter Stevens.

Stevens, at his drum kit, was supposed to be the leader. 'I'm supposed to be the leader!' he was yelling. 'You're supposed to be playing what I'm playing.'

'What are you playing, then?' Michael Bradshaw was shouting at him.

'They sound better now,' Beccs said.

'Yeah,' I said. 'I reckon we could do better than that.'

'We could look a whole lot better, too,' Kirsty said.

Which was a dead typical thing for her to say. You wouldn't know she was Becca's cousin. Beccs isn't tall, only about ten centimetres taller than me. She is a bit, not fat, but not not fat, if you know what I mean. While Kirsten is nearly two metres long with legs that could stretch the length of about Becca's and my own added together. She is, Kirsty I mean, drop-dead gorgeous; but, you know, I wasn't the only one, I'm sure, who thought she would be a lot more gorgeous still if she really did drop dead. I sometimes thought of suggesting it to her; worth a try, I thought. She'd do practically anything if she thought it made her look good.

'We could look a whole lot better than those grunge,' Kirsty was saying, nodding towards the three boys as they started playing three different songs simultaneously.

'That was much better,' Peter Stevens said, when the racket collapsed again after a few seconds or so. 'At least we all started at the same time that time.'

'W-what s-song were we playing?' Geoffrey Fryer said.

'Don't you know?' Stevens asked.

'Do you?' Geoffrey Fryer asked back.

'Course I do!' he shouted.

'Yeah,' Bradshaw butted in, 'of course you do. Cause every one's the same for you. You just do the same thing, whatever we're supposed to be playing.'

'S-so do I,' said Geoffrey Fryer, laughing nervously.

He was laughing because we were. We were creasing up. They were pathetic, hopeless. Rehearsals to them meant practising all starting at the same time. None of them could play. Peter Stevens couldn't sing to save his life. Which never really mattered, as they never seemed to get anywhere near that far. Nobody ever knew what The Grunge Machine were supposed to sound like.

'They're rubbish,' Beccs was shouting as we ran out with our hands over our ears.

'Wassamatter, girls?' Stevens was calling after us. 'Don't you like Blur, or something?'

'W-were we d-d-doing Blur?' long Geoffrey Fryer was shouting over the ear-pierce of feedback through the amps.

'They were blurred, anyway,' I tried to say.

'What do you mean?' Kirsty said, looking down at me.

I always felt that Kirsty was looking down at me. She was, being about a good thirty centimetres taller than me; but especially as she was always asking me when I was going to have another fit. 'We could all see the state of your knickers, don't worry,' she told me last time I had a seizure in one of the corridors, as if she'd enjoyed it. I was supposed to always take different tablets twice a day and eat regularly and everything, but sometimes forgot. I hated it, but I think Kirsten was a bit jealous of the fact that I could do something as glamorous and mysterious as having an epileptic fit in front of everybody. I think she envied me the attention it always brought, never mind about my own shame and embarrassment at being so far out of control.

'What do you mean?' she said, pretending not to understand what I'd said about The Grunge Machine being blurred.

'Joke,' I said.

'Joke?' she said, with that dim, puzzled look she always put on her face. 'I never get your jokes. Do you ever get Amy's jokes?' she said to Beccs.

Becca just laughed. She didn't think anything was funny, but was laughing because she didn't want to be put on the spot.

'You're just thick,' I said to Kirsty.

4

'Ooh,' Kirsty said, 'listen to the maths professor. You think everyone's thick, just because no one can understand anything you say.'

'Don't start arguing, you two,' Beccs had to step in and say. She was always having to step in between us. I wished she'd never had a cousin, then long tall Kirsten wouldn't *be* her cousin and wouldn't have to hang round with us with her long hair and long legs and short skirts.

'I'm not arguing,' Kirsty said, flicking her hair in that way she had, when she wanted to be better, or at least hairier, than everybody else. She flicked her hair in a different way whenever she wanted to be noticed.

I noticed she'd gone from flicking her hair one way to flicking it the other when Ben Lyons, who had come to the school from trouble in London, or so the rumours said, at the beginning of his Year Thirteen, came round the corner on his own. He was nearly always on his own; not because he had to be, but because he wanted it like that. He wouldn't have been on his own for a minute if half the girls in our school had anything to do with it. It was ridiculous, the way they all went silent and stupid whenever he was around, talking about him all the time when he wasn't, or pretending they didn't like him when everyone could see they did.

Kirsty went quiet as soon as he appeared in the corridor going in the opposite direction to the three of us. Kirsty's hair was being flicked in her 'notice-me, notice-me' mode, as she forgot all about what she'd been saying to me.

In fact, we all went quiet as he came towards us. I think I could feel Becca's heart rate, going thick and fast by my side. It could have been my own, maybe. I didn't think so though. I wasn't like that. I was the Grade-A Maths and Physics student; Maths and Physics just weren't like that.

Actually, I was studying A-Level Biology, too. So maybe,

5

just maybe that was what I could feel. Maybe I could feel my biology quickening as Ben Lyons approached. I don't know. Maybe.

I was going to say something to him, really I was; but I had such a dry mouth, I had to rely upon Beccs to get in before Kirsten could make us look like three sweet-toothed girlie-girls.

But: 'Hi, Ben,' she managed to giggle first, while Beccs and me were swallowing hard on nothing. Kirsty's long blonde hair was swishing over our heads like some kind of boy-beacon to be seen for miles all round.

'Hi,' Ben said.

We all stopped, with nothing to say between us. Ben was looking at us in turn. Kirsten was pushing back her hair, trying to push herself forward.

'You been to see the band?' Ben said.

'Yeah,' Beccs finally managed to say. I'd never seen her like this before. Beccs was a football player. She went around telling everyone she played for Man U and England when she wasn't at school doing her A-Levels. She always went round out of school kitted out in a M.U.F.C. home or away strip, including the socks. She had a dog at home called Victoria and a real leather football signed by the whole of the first team of only two seasons ago. She played the beautiful game better than most boys in our year and was in the school team. First girl ever. She was fast and furious and deadly accurate; and stood there just behind her long tall cousin like a poor cousin herself, ashamed of her player's legs and grazed knees.

'Is that where you're going?' Kirsty quickly asked.

'Yeah,' he said. 'Thought I'd check them out.'

'Don't bother,' I managed to say. He looked at me, as if he'd only just noticed I was down there. I know I'm not a

6

metre and a half tall or anything, but I'm not *that* small. 'They're rubbish,' I said.

He smiled. Kirsten looked over me.

'They're called The Grunge Machine,' I said. 'Have you ever heard such a rubbish name for a band?'

Ben gave a little laugh.

'Yeah,' I said, 'they're into rubbish copies of Blur but all out of synch with each other, all starting on different tunes at different times.'

'Yeah,' Ben said, 'I know what you mean. Like, really blurred,' he said.

We were all laughing together then, at Ben's little joke; except that Kirsten, when I looked at her, had some kind of a nasty smell under her nose, judging by the look on her face.

'Amy said that,' Beccs said.

Ben looked at me again.

'Amy reckons she could do better herself,' Kirsty said, as the laughter began to fade.

'Your name Amy?' Ben said to me.

I nodded.

'Mine's –'

'Rebecca,' Ben interrupted her by saying. 'I know. I've seen you play. You're good.'

'Thanks,' Beccs said, her face reddening. Actually reddening! I'd never once seen her blush before.

'And you already know my name,' Kirsten told Ben, as sweet as you like.

'Yeah,' Ben said, but not convincingly enough not to make Kirsten feel uncomfortable.

'Kirsty,' she said.

'Yeah,' Ben said. 'You can sing, then?' he said, to me.

'Better than that lot, I can,' I said, indicating back towards the hall.

'Why don't we give it a try then?' he said, just like that.

'What,' Beccs said, after a long while in which we all stood looking at each other, 'just like that?'

'Yeah,' Ben laughed. 'Just like that. Why not?'

We laughed.

'Why not?' Ben said again.

Again we all laughed.

'I've got some tunes,' he said. 'Why don't we give it a go?'

Beccs and I were looking at each other, both wondering if he was having us on.

'Well I will,' Kirsty said, swaying forward. 'I've always wanted to be a singer. My mum says I look like –'

'And what about you two?' Ben said, to Beccs and me.

We looked at each other again and smiled. 'Nah!' we both said, simultaneously.

'Great timing,' Ben laughed. 'Perfect pitch. But where were you?' he said to Kirsty. She shuffled.

'What was your name again?' Ben said to her, as she flicked back her hair.

✳✳✳Two

My mum was pulling her hair out when I got home. 'At last!' she shouted at me as soon as I came through the door. 'I didn't know you were going to be late home tonight. Where have you been?'

'Just out with Beccs and –'

'I'm so late. Your tea's out there. Georgina's in the dining room watching a video. Take your tea in there. Okay? Amy? Okay?'

'Yes. All right!'

'I'm so late!'

'Then go.'

'I don't know where your father is. He promised me. You'd think he'd keep a promise, once in a while, wouldn't you? I needed his car. Mine keeps cutting out. I'll have to risk it. Oh no! Is that the time?'

My mum was supposed to be learning yoga. She was supposed to go to the Adult Education Centre, which is, actually, my school, three or four times a week to learn about yoga, reiki, acupuncture, all sorts of things, exercises and breathing techniques for meditating and being calm.

'I'm always late!' she was shrieking, looking everywhere for her car keys. 'Every week I'm the last one to arrive. When I get there – have you seen my keys? – they've always started and I have to meditate like mad to try and catch up.'

She was running round the house, looking in the loo and

the fridge for her car keys. 'That father of yours! You tell him, when he gets home. Whenever that is. You tell him. It's not fair. Go and see if Georgie's got my keys. Have a look in her nappy for me, would you?'

As soon as I opened the door on her, Georgina screamed at me over the noise of her full-volumed video, struggling from a juddering high chair. She reached out for me, dragging at my shirt front.

Mum came in while we were wrestling on the carpet. 'It's all right. I've found them,' she said, picking them out of a pile of baked beans heaped on the carpet in front of the TV set. 'George!' she shouted.

Georgie was hanging onto the front of me, squeezing my nose.

'Georgie! Where's the rest of your dinner? – Amy, be a love and try and find the rest of Georgie's dinner, would you? Can you try to make sure she's eaten some?'

Georgina had beans in her hair. Now they were all over my clothes. 'Mum! Why'd you leave her with it?'

'I forgot. I've got to go, okay? Do what you can. Your father should be home soon.'

I was trying to get the beans and sausage out of Georgie's hair when my mother appeared again, wiping her keys with a paper towel. 'Have you done your homework?' she called. 'Did you take your tablets? Do your homework,' calling out to me as she slammed the front door closed.

Georgina, hearing the door go, started to scream. She always screamed when someone went out of the house. She always screamed whenever anyone came in. So did her twin sister, Joanna – Jo. Georgie also cried whenever Jo did. Jo did whenever George did: as she did right then, from upstairs. I had to go up and get her out of her cot. She smiled when she saw me, but screamed again when she saw little Georgie downstairs with beans and sausages tied to her hair. Jo wanted beans and sausages for *her* hair.

I had to go into the kitchen and fetch my own tea from the cooker for their cheeks and their hair and for the floor and my clothes. We were always having food fights in our house, every day. Every day my dad was stomping out of the house with sloppy rusk ground into his business suit. His ties were all stained with milk-sick. And that was just him. My mum was almost permanently coated in yoghurt, with the smell of gripe-water and liquefied banana hanging round her like a cloud.

So there I was, combing the sausages out of my baby sisters' hair all evening waiting for my dad to come home, when I should have been studying for my A-Level Maths. I was trying to dig the beans out of the carpet and find a Teletubbies video to distract my twin sisters when I should have been trying to understand why, in differential calculus, when you differentiated the trigonometrical function of the sine wave you got a cosine wave. Can somebody explain that to me, please? No?

They're still babies yet, my little sisters. They're fourteen years younger than me, which was a bit of a surprise, to everyone. Not least my mum. She thought she couldn't get pregnant any more. My dad thought so too. I know this, because I had to listen to them both arguing about it for the nine months until the twins came.

But they're still babies; they don't know yet what a pair of Peppercorns they are. I kept getting stuck with them as they mashed beans into each other's hair and made each other cry and took it in turns to pop with sick. They were having a good scream and one of them was going red in the face, making a rare stink in her nappy when I was late home from school from watching the worst band in the world when I should have been doing my maths.

I tried to get my books out and at least have a look at the explanation on the differentiation of trigonometric functions. Don't you know what I'm talking about? No? You and me both. Maths wasn't so bad last term, at GCSE level; I quite enjoyed messing about with numbers. There was something satisfying about it, when you got the answer you were looking for and you understood why. I always thought I could see why maths worked, by representations of the problem and its solution in my mind, like a maths picture only I could see and fully appreciate. There was something of myself in it; I could identify with it.

But now – we've just started at A-Level, and this differential of sine x is equal to cosine x, it means nothing to me. I have no pictures for it. I could open my books at the appropriate page and there was an explanation in black and white, but written, colourlessly, picturelessly, drying my brains to a crisp frazzle. I couldn't think about it.

A flop of semi-masticated beans slopped across the open pages of my books. I had the twins in their twin high chairs, from where they were throwing mashed beans in a tomato and spit sauce from a secret supply I had failed to discover. The Teletubbies were doing one of their little dances as I did one of mine. 'Look at my books,' I was screeching as I danced about, looking for a tissue. 'You two! – Oh, Dad, where are you?'

I was always getting collared, coerced into looking after my very little sisters because no one in this house could be bothered. It wasn't fair. It wasn't my fault. I didn't want my parents to have any more kids. Neither did they, evidently; but they went and did it, not me. I was just a kid myself. I was supposed to be studying, but I was dancing out into the kitchen for some paper towels and howling to the moon while my sisters were screeching and packing their nappies in front of the Teletubbies. The house was in a drastic mess, with unwashed washing-up in the bowl and piles of laundry and no paper tissues for my beaned-up books.

I was running upstairs for some loo paper, when I heard the front door slam above the racket the twins were now making, and my dad's voice bellowing up after me, making the twins scream all the louder. 'Where are you?' he stood roaring, until I appeared running down the stairs with half a roll of paper wrapped round my left hand.

'What are you doing to these two?' he wanted to know, glaring at me, at the twins, back at me. 'What's going on, for pity's sake? Where's your m – Oh no! What day is it?'

'Yoga,' I said, wiping the pages of my maths books. 'You were supposed to be home early.'

'Can't you shut those two up?' he raged.

We were both having to shout over the noise of Georgie and Jo, as they tried to give The Grunge Machine a run for their money. They were doing pretty good too, considering they were ampless, acoustic, unplugged.

'What's the matter with them?'

'They want changing.'

'I know,' he shouted. 'I'd change them for a new car, I would. I'd change them for an *old* car. I'd change them for anything. What's happening in this house? Is this what I always have to come home to?'

'Dad, I've got to do my home –'

'You can't leave me with these two. They stink. Amy, I need your help. I'm sorry. This isn't fair, is it?'

'No,' I said, as we lifted a twin each from the high chairs, 'no, it isn't.'

'No,' he said. 'I shouldn't have to come home to all this.

We haven't been here all day, have we? We have to go out all day. Surely there's enough time to sort this place, during the day? Wouldn't you think?'

'I don't know, Dad. I don't know.'

✳✳✳ Three

'**I** know you're trying to break up The Grunge,' Peter Stevens came over and said to Beccs and me. 'I know what you're trying to do.'

'What you taking about?' Beccs said.

'You and her. The football player and the midget.'

'Hey,' Beccs said, leaping to attention. 'Watch your mouth, Stevens!'

'No,' he said, 'you're right, I'm sorry. You're no kind of a football player, are you. You're just a wannabe bloke.'

'And you're just a rubbish drummer,' I said, 'who can't sing.'

'Yeah,' he said, 'I know you think you can do better. I'll wait and see. I'll be laughing, then, I tell you.' He started to walk away. 'The Grunge Machine can do without Geoffrey Fryer, anyway. You can have him. He's just a liability.'

'What was that all about?' Beccs said.

'I dunno,' I said, 'but I think we should go and find your cousin, before Stevens does.'

I was saying that, saying we needed to find Kirsten before Stevens did, not because I was worried what he might say to her, but because of what I thought she'd already started saying to him. His remarks had her stamp all over them. That stuff about me thinking I could do better than some grunge-indie band, that was straight from the horse's mouth.

'I haven't been speaking to Peter Stevens,' Kirsty said, with

15

an expression of sweet innocence that would melt no butter.

I didn't believe her. 'What's all this stuff about Geoffrey Fryer, as well?'

'Don't ask me,' she said.

'She doesn't know anything,' Beccs said.

I knew she did though. She had that look about her. I could see it. Beccs never could. She could never see what a scheming and jealous little cow – big cow – her cousin was. I was always forced to play the politician, keeping my mouth shut when I had something to say, or saying it diplomatically, couching it in terms that couldn't offend; or not very often, anyway. In this way, I was as conniving as Kirsten herself, the two of us playing a game of hit and run round her cousin and my best friend.

But then I'd get bored with the game. I'd want to tell Kirsty what a piece of lank string she was and how she made everyone fed up with just being in her company. Then Becca would have to step in to keep the peace and Kirsty would go all innocent and victimised and I'd feel another wedge driven between myself and the best friend I'd had ever since I could remember.

Kirsten was always hanging round us. I didn't know why. Well, I did, but I couldn't discuss it with Beccs. They're first cousins, close family, so I can't tell my best friend that her cousin was only with us because she didn't have anybody else. No one else liked her, not since Melanie Cox, who used to be Kirsten's best, and only, friend, drank three bottles of alco-orange and decided that Kirsty needed a few hard truths bringing home. Now they hate each other, and Mel Cox's new best mate hates Kirsty too.

They all used to hate us in those days, but we didn't care. Beccs didn't care, even though Kirsten was her first cousin.

We were good mates, Beccs and me; so the others didn't matter in the least.

Then Kirsten started coming round, calling on her cousin and trying to get in with her. I still didn't like her; neither did Beccs, I was sure; but family's family, I suppose.

'Or,' Kirsty said, 'it might be something to do with our new band.'

Beccs and I stood blinking up at her. I knew she knew something, the way she swayed, swishing her hair behind her back like the tail of a real pony. She was so sweet, so innocent. So very conniving.

'Ben Lyons is serious,' she said. She was trying not to smile too broadly. 'He came and – actually, he came looking for me, to tell me his idea.'

'What idea?' Beccs said.

'Well,' Kirsty said, addressing herself directly to her cousin, as if I didn't enter into it, 'Ben says he thinks we'll all look pretty cool fronting his new band if I'm in the middle, with you on one side,' she said to Beccs, 'and you on the other,' she nodded briefly at me, 'with him on drum machine and mixer. Then all we need is someone on keyboards.'

'That's all we need, is it?' I said.

'He doesn't even know if we can sing,' Beccs said.

'No,' Kirsty said, 'but we'll look good, and that's nearly all there is to it, isn't it?'

Beccs and I looked at each other. 'I thought we said no,' I said.

'Ben doesn't take no for an answer,' Kirsty said. 'He's so insistent. He really wants us to do it.'

'Well I'm not doing it,' Beccs said.

'No,' I said, 'neither am I. And that's all there is to it.'

It wasn't, of course. There was plenty more to it than that.

You wouldn't be here now if it was, neither would I. But you are, and so am I.

Ben Lyons looked at me when we, Beccs and me, went to him with every intention of demanding to know who he thought he was, insisting that we were going to be singers in his band when we'd said absolutely not.

'We didn't say we would,' I said, trying not to stammer as he looked at me. He had this way of gazing at you that disarmed all your demands, taking the edge off your insistence, until you were left not quite sure what you really wanted or what you'd actually said.

'We didn't say we'd sing,' I was saying, quite unsure of myself now, and quite disconcerted that he could do this to me, make me feel like this. I mean, it wasn't as if I really liked him or anything.

'We didn't say we would,' Beccs said, 'so we won't.' She sounded much more resolved than I did, much more in control. Her face, however, as I glanced at her, glowed as if she'd just won a really tough match.

He was looking at us, disconcerting both of us, before he shrugged and said, 'So what you sending your tall mate round for?'

'What do you mean?' Beccs asked.

Ben's eyes fixed upon her. I felt her make some kind of reaction to him from beside me. I don't know what she did, but I felt something.

'I mean,' he said, smiling, I'm sure, at her reaction to him, 'your mate Kirsty coming after me asking what we're going to do about the band and who's going to be lead singer and who else is going to be in it and a thousand other things? How'm I supposed to know?'

Beccs and I were looking at each other.

'She told me,' Ben was saying, to Beccs, 'that you're in,' then saying, 'and you're out.'

'Well I'm not either,' Beccs said.

I felt good when she said that, going against her cousin and everything.

'She said you're too little,' Ben Lyons was saying to me, ignoring Beccs for the minute. 'She said you'd look like a little boy on the stage. She said you sang like one, too. Like a choirboy, she said.'

'She was joking,' Beccs said.

'Was she?' Ben said, looking at me. 'Don't you sing like a choirboy then?'

'She was joking,' Beccs said again. 'Amy can sing better than any of us. Kirsty knows that. These two are always winding each other up,' she said.

'I don't care,' Ben shrugged. 'I don't have a problem finding girls.'

'No,' I said, 'we know.'

He looked at me again, in that disconcerting way.

'No,' Beccs said, coming to my rescue. 'So you'd better go and find some others, because we aren't doing it, are we Amy?'

'No,' I said. 'Definitely not. Even if I am the best singer in the school.'

'Well, I heard you had a voice,' Ben said.

'Did you?' I said.

'Did you?' said Beccs, as if Ben had been talking to her.

'Yeah,' he said. 'Shame to waste it. Still, if your mind's made up?'

'It is,' Beccs said. 'Isn't it, Amy?'

'Yeah,' I said. 'Definitely.'

'Definitely,' said Beccs.

'Definitely,' we were saying, as Ben Lyons looked at us, disconcerting us into feeling not very definite at all.

So we were not going to turn up at Ben Lyons's first rehearsal in the hall on Friday evening. Definitely not, however bad he made us feel about turning him down. Most of the girls in our school would have jumped at the chance, I knew; but I had enough to worry about, without thinking of singing in some useless band in front of everyone I knew and making an idiot of myself. Kirsten could do it, if she liked. Beccs didn't want to do it, me neither. Kirsten wasn't part of our decision on this one. I liked that. Beccs wanted what I did, without her cousin; she could make an idiot of herself by herself. Yes, she definitely could make an idiot of herself. She was good at that.

I am a good singer though. I've always had a voice. I'm quite little, as I said, but I've got a big voice. I'd always sung to my baby sisters in their twin high chairs to shut them up. I was louder than they were, so where they wouldn't keep quiet for another Tinkie-TV session, they'd often shut up for me. I used to do this really old song my mum always liked me singing. I don't know anything about the song, or how I came to know it so well, but I knew it all the way through:

You would seize the day for me,
Keep the night away for me,
Make the darkness light for me,
The noble sun ignite for me,
If ever, if ever you were here . . .

A really old song, very sad with a big tune, but, you know, good to sing when you've got a voice.

The twins would be wailing in their chairs, throwing plates and crying, my mum would be throwing plates into the sink, and crying, and I'd start to sing to quieten the lot of them in one go. 'You would seize the day for me,' and I'd look and the twins would be watching me and my mum would be sucking a dummy, quite forgetting to put it into one open and dribbling baby-mouth or the other.

So it was nearly every morning after my dad had rushed out protecting his newly cleaned suit from the food flying across our kitchen; as it was that morning, the morning of Ben's first rehearsal. My mum was breathing like a yoga addict, trying to relax after another bust with my dad. He'd been sitting at the kitchen table trying to read his paper, with a twin on either side of him tugging at his news headlines and sports reviews left and right.

'Why?' my mum was asking, scraping the burnt eggs out of the frying pan.

'Because I don't like burnt eggs,' my dad was saying. His name's Tony, by the way. Anthony Peppercorn. He was a Peppercorn before any of us.

My mum used to be called Jill Tidy. But now she's a Peppercorn too, and tidy she is not. Not any longer. Jill Peppercorn is now very un-Tidy. She worries about her heart rate. She worries about relaxation so much she can't relax. She worries about worrying so much. Sometimes her teeth ache she worries so much. She was studying yoga and reiki, aromatherapy, acupuncture and wine tasting.

My dad tasted wine, too. He had to work late all the time, but when he came home he often smelled like half a bottle of Beaujolais and a big fat cigar.

Mum burned the eggs again. The toast was cold, we were all late and the twins were wet and filthy from the print off the broadsheet they'd stolen and sucked into papier-mâché.

21

'I don't like burnt eggs.'

The twins' mouths looked blackened with burnt egg white and news headlines. I opened my school bag and a great fat sausage of masticated newspaper flopped straight into it.

'No,' my mum was saying, 'I mean, why have you got to be late home again tonight?'

'Work,' my dad simply said. 'Just work.'

'But you're always so late home nowdays. And in a few weeks, you'll be away for the whole weekend and –'

'I told you,' he said, 'there are a lot of changes coming up. We're all pushed to our limit. Everyone's up to their eyes in it. Look at this paper now. I wanted that to read on the train.'

'Angela's husband works in the city,' my mum was saying.

My dad looked up. 'What's that got to do with anything?'

'He works in financial services, like you. He doesn't have to work all hours like you do, or go away on any –'

'I don't – what's that got to do with anything? What are you saying?'

'I'm not saying anything. I just –'

'You just like making irrelevant comparisons.'

'No. I just – Amy, I bet your friends at school don't all have fathers coming home all hours, do they?'

'No,' my father answered. 'But I bet at least some of them do, don't they, Amy? Because that's how it is, for some of us. Isn't it, Amy?'

'Is it, Amy?' my mum was asking.

They had a row once, my mum and dad; it started when my mum surprised everyone by falling pregnant, and is still continuing. When they found out it was twins, you could have hacked through the shocked silence in this house with a rusty butter knife. Then the screaming started. It has never stopped.

They stood over me in the kitchen, asking me to resolve

their problems for them. They were always trying to get me to decide. I could never say anything. I couldn't resolve a problem if it was written down in black and white with an explanation and several examples in a maths book.

My mum had always helped me with my maths. She had been a teacher once, a good one, before she became the mother of twins. My father, before he was father to his baby daughters, was happy being an ambitionless small office worker and husband to a first class teacher. 'I'm forty-seven next birthday,' I'd hear him wail as my maths problems eluded me night after night.

'Well so am I!' my mother would start back at him. She could handle a full class of secondary school nutcases with ease day after day, but couldn't stand to have his and her own age shouted again into her face.

She had tried to persuade my dad to give up work for a few years to look after the twins. She had tried to persuade me to persuade him. He wouldn't do it. He couldn't.

'What do you think I am?' he shouted.

'What does she think I am?' he appealed to me.

'Well what does he think *I* am?' she turned to me and said. She was heavily pregnant at the time.

Do you know what it's like when you're nearly fourteen and your mum's well into her forties and that big with pregnancy? It is *so* embarrassing. All your mates can see what's happening. They look at you as if they're wondering why. The thing is, was, I never did know why. Nobody did. That's why there was so much arguing, so many angry silences, pregnant pauses that were set to last the full nine months and way beyond.

The thing is, was, my mum wasn't right for staying at home all day every day. My dad was all wrong for the new job he

23

got in the city to earn more money to make up for the loss of my mum's wages. I was never supposed to have these parents that weren't right for the lives they were leading, or being led by. I wanted help with my homework, my maths. They thought I wanted to become a doctor one day. I don't know, I can't remember what made them think so; maybe when I was little I played at being a doctor, so they thought I wanted to be one. But I don't know what there was in it to make my parents take me so seriously. I didn't want to be a doctor, as much as my mum didn't want to be a housewife, or my dad a financial services executive. I didn't want to do A-Level Maths and Physics, or Biology. I'd got off on a wrong foot to please them, I knew already, at the start of the first term; but they never noticed.

My dad was too busy being harassed from the house and into the train without his newspaper. My mum was just too busy being harassed. The eggs were burnt, the toast cold and the twins screaming to get out of their twin high chairs and start deconstructing the house again. I hadn't a hope of understanding trigonometrical differentiation, so sang my song, the only one I knew all the way through.

'You would seize the day for me,' I sang, in my big voice, standing to my full height of one metre and a whole forty-seven centimetres.

You would seize the day for me,
Keep the night away for me,
Make the darkness light for me,
The noble sun ignite for me,
If ever, if ever you were here.

And if ever you were here again
I'd never shed a tear again
Or make the sunrise mine alone

Or see a new sun shine alone
If ever, if ever you were here . . .

One metre forty-seven centimetres tall. Short, but in proportion. If you saw a picture of me, a photograph, and I wasn't standing next to a chair or beside a door or anything, you wouldn't be able to tell how small I am. If everyone else in a photo were to stand about three metres behind me, you'd never know. We'd all look the same size. But we're not. I'm little, but with a voice that filled the kitchen far more than my body could, quietening the twins to a dribble from their almost matching open mouths and eliciting a quiet tear from my mother. 'I love it when you sing that song,' she said, as soon as I stopped singing that song; as soon as I did stop singing, or shortly after at least, the twins started up again and I had to gather my stuff and get ready to leave for school.

'I've always loved it when you sing that song,' my mother sniffed. She was crying. The twins were crying.

'I – er – might be a bit – late –'

'Oh no!' she cried. 'I've got reiki. You're not going to be late home again, are you? *He'll* be late again, no doubt. It isn't fair. I'll be late again and miss everything again. Do you have to be late? Can you not – no, you go and – *he* should be here. He should, shouldn't he? I wish someone could make him see how unfair it always is,' she said, looking at me, as I was someone, anyone, at all.

We weren't going, Beccs and me. No way. We weren't going to subject ourselves to that. Just – no way!

We went, anyway. Well, we had to see what Ben Lyons was

25

going to do, didn't we? We couldn't just not go; not after he'd specifically asked us, could we?

'I'm not interested in him,' I said to Beccs, 'are you?'

'No,' she said, changing the subject quickly, too quickly, by telling me about some new fad diet she was thinking of trying. Ever since her cousin Kirsten had gatecrashed our scene, Beccs was always going on about different diets. She was a football player, probably the best girl player in the county. She played for the school and was supposed to be going for a trial for the Arsenal Ladies Under 18s. That was before the imposition of Kirsten. There was a before-Kirsten Beccs, and an after-Kirsten Rebecca. And I knew, beyond a shadow of a doubt, which version I preferred.

She was a bit, not fat, but not *not* fat, as I said; which had always been all right by her, and by me. She was much, much faster than she looked, even stronger than she looked; and, I tell you, could she ever kick a ball? She was a midfielder, with a hard and accurate kick. She practised placing the ball, centimetre-perfect, from metres outside the penalty area. She was the free-kick king – queen – king; of course she was: she was Beccs, with a dog at home called Vicky and a whole barrelful of real girl-power.

But that was the pre-Kirsten version. Now fad diets kept coming and going, ruining Becca's training programme by taking away nearly all her energy and her power and her speed. She was becoming less comfortable with being a football player, I could tell. Kirsten kept on and on trying to girlify Beccs. She wasn't the same any more. The other Saturday I saw the two of them, Kirsty and Beccs, in the mall at the shopping centre, with Kirsty in a pair of hipster trousers and a tiny top, but with Beccs – wearing a skirt. A skirt, on a Saturday! Beccs in a short skirt with Man U set to line up against Liverpool at home! Man U had got The Pool away, and Beccs was wandering about in the mall in the shortest skirt I'd ever seen her wearing, ever!

Her big knees had Kirsten's influence written all over them, even more clearly than the scabs on her grazes. It made me feel really strange seeing them there in the mall on a Saturday afternoon like that. I had to dodge back into one of the shops so that they didn't see me. I grabbed something from the skirt rack and went to the back of the shop pretending I wanted to try it on. I sat in the changing cubicle on my own wondering why Beccs had told me she was staying in that afternoon to do some schoolwork and to catch the football results as they came in.

I didn't wonder about it for long. I knew that my mate Beccs was turning more and more into the Becky-girl her first cousin wanted as a friend. My first friend Beccs had lied to me so that she could go out like a Becky wearing a skirt instead of her away strip without having to be embarrassed about it. It made me feel very strange to think about the fact that my best friend was more comfortable and having more fun with someone like Kirsten than she would be with me. And that she didn't know I knew.

'No, I'm not interested in him,' Beccs said to me, the day of the evening we definitely weren't going to see Ben Lyons putting his band together in the hall, before changing the subject too quickly.

It didn't sound like the truth to me now. So much of what she said made me wonder what she said when she was with Kirsten. Becca certainly wasn't behaving as if she really didn't have any interest in Ben. She blushed for him, making the lie that she was telling me that much more obvious. She was interested in him. So was Kirsten. But Kirsten didn't lie about it like Beccs; she just fancied him, as simply as that.

I was the only one, as far as I could tell, who was genuinely

27

uninterested in Ben Lyons. He made me feel a bit, kind of, wobbly, especially when he looked at me, but what of it? That didn't mean anything. I really couldn't have cared less if I never saw him again for the rest of my life. All the girls fancied him. He made them all feel the same, when he looked at them. I just didn't want to be like everyone else, that's all. And if I did feel the same as all the others, I certainly didn't want to give Ben Lyons the satisfaction of showing it.

That's why I definitely wasn't going to the hall to make myself look a fool in front of any pee-taking Peter Stevens or anybody else with a grunge-grudge and a grinning, mocking sense of humour. 'No way,' I said to Beccs.

'Nor me,' she agreed. 'No way.'

Stevens was there, of course, at the back of the hall with his grin in place and primed for use against us as soon as we got there. Skinny Geoffrey Fryer, ex-Grunge Mechanic, was up on the stage with Ben, flapping nervously over his keyboard and glancing again and again at Stevens up the back.

'Here comes the talent!' Stevens shouted, as Kirsty, Beccs and I filed past in that order, shortening drastically as we went.

'Where?' his mate, the other grungster Michael Bradshaw said, from where he sat crumpled into one of the furthest away chairs. 'Talent?' Bradshaw said, his head popping up between the lines of seats. 'I can't see no talent.'

'No,' said Stevens. 'On second thoughts, neither can I.'

We filed past them in as I said, descending height-order, with no words to say in our defence. I don't know about the others – well, I do; they were like me – and I was feeling like a complete idiot and wishing I'd kept to my word.

Geoffrey Fryer was twittering away, fiddling with every-thing at once, looking and not looking. But Ben Lyons was definitely not looking. He was going through papers and notes and stuff he had in some rat-eaten folder, taking no notice of anything at all as if he really wasn't expecting anyone else to turn up.

I was feeling more and more stupid as we made our way to the front of the hall. Ben Lyons was taking no notice of us at all. We'd told him we weren't going to be there; we shouldn't have been there.

Kirsty and Beccs were feeling foolish too, I could tell. We were all slowing down as we approached the stage, looking up at Ben and Geoffrey like imbeciles as Geoffrey smiled at us and laughed and looked at Ben and stopped laughing. He looked at us again, and started laughing again. Ben was still shuffling pages, apparently oblivious to us.

Kirsten's hair was flying: 'Notice me! Notice me!' Beccs, I could feel, I could actually feel without looking, was blistering beetroot red. We had to stand together looking up expectantly, like no-hopers no one wanted to pick for their team.

'Well,' I said, after far too long a silence from Kirsten and Beccs, 'we're here.'

'Right,' Ben Lyons looked up without a glimmer of surprise or welcome, 'good. Now we can do some stuff,' he said, tapping together his papers.

So we stood there, we three girls, with Geoffrey Fryer nervously glancing to the back at the other Grunge Machine members and Ben Lyons looking up casually at us with his eyebrows raised, saying, 'Well?'

We seemed to shuffle closer together as he looked at us, with Kirsten's hair flying above our heads like a comfort blanket.

'What can you do?' Ben said.

'Do?' I said.

'We can do Courtney Schaeffer,' Kirsten suddenly spurted out.

'Really?' Ben said, with some kind of mock amusement on his face. 'What a surprise.'

'*Survive*,' said Kirsty.

Ben nodded. '*Survive*.'

'I can't,' I said. 'I don't know it.'

'We do though,' Kirsty said, 'don't we, Becky?'

Beccs took a sidelong, embarrassed glance at me. 'Yes,' she said, too quietly, as if she didn't want me to hear her admission. Admitting that she and Kirsten knew *Survive* by Courtney Schaeffer all the way through, was the same as admitting they'd been rehearsing it together.

'Okay,' Ben said, 'let's hear you and Becky do it then. Come up here on the stage. Me and Geoff will go down there.'

'Yeah,' the grunge merchants up the back were calling. 'Here we go.'

'I can't,' Beccs said. 'Not with those two up there. Not like that.'

'What,' Ben said, looking back at Peter Stevens and Michael Bradshaw, 'those two? They're no bother.'

'They are,' Geoffrey said softly.

'See,' said Beccs.

Ben smiled. He looked to the back of the hall. 'Would you two mind leaving?' he called. 'The girls here want to do a kind of non-swimmer's version of *Survive*.'

'Yes,' Stevens called back, 'we would.'

Ben looked down at us. He shrugged. 'They would mind, apparently. What can I do? They're an audience. That's what it's all about, girls. Take it or leave it.' And he offered them the stage with a very stagy flourish.

So Kirsty and Beccs shuffled sheepishly up the few steps to the stage as Geoffrey gratefully whipped down them, followed by a mockingly amused Ben Lyons. Up they loped, abashed and ashamed by the laughter from the back of the hall.

'We can't just do it,' Beccs said, 'with no music or any-thing.'

'Why not?' Ben asked.

'Come on,' Kirsty said. 'Let's just be Courtney. I'll be her, right, and you can be –'

'And I'll be all the others,' Beccs said, with a little more of the footballer's spirit back with her. Kirsten looked at her. 'Joke,' Beccs said.

'Oh,' said Kirsten. 'Right. – Ready?'

'No,' said Beccs. 'I can't do it.'

The boys up the back were laughing louder.

'Course you can,' said Kirsten. 'Just follow me.' And she launched herself into the song from the beginning and ran through to the end doing a clumsy copy of the dances from the video, with my poor friend Beccs doing an even poorer copy just behind her.

Poor Beccs. Kirsty had been practising for this, anybody could see. She'd obviously been roping Becca in, learning the video actions bit by bit in preparation for her big audition.

The boys up the back were having a great time as Beccs missed a great chunk of the lyric and went off into the verse, stomping up the stage trying to be a survivor while her cousin tried to survive the ordeal herself by hauling her back. Becca didn't once look in my direction. She couldn't look at me.

I was squirming in my seat next to Ben, embarrassed for my friend. The whole thing was horrible, copying the actions and expressions from a pop video like a couple of teeny-teens shouting 'girl-power' as a means of expressing their 'individu-ality'. It all had that kind of silly wannabe flavour to it, from their flat bumpy voices to their long school socks and black

31

shoes. I could feel, I swear, Ben Lyons gritting his teeth beside me. I could hear the sound of my own teeth grinding inside my head.

It went on a long, long time before the toe-curling finale that left Kirsten posing and pouting like Courtney Schaeffer herself and Beccs making a break for it down the stairs from the stage. The grunge-boys were shouting and cheering for less, much less.

Beccs ran to one of the seats on the far side of Geoffrey Fryer, who was frozen into a grinning stick of something like disbelief, and buried her head in her hands. 'I knew we shouldn't,' I could hear Beccs repeating over and over. 'I knew we shouldn't.'

Kirsten, meanwhile, was stepping down from the stage as if she had just been presented with an award at the Brits. She was smiling. Her full hair was going from side to side. 'Well?' she said to Ben. 'What did you think? Will we do?'

I detected that even Ben had dropped a bit of his cool. 'It –' he said, searching for words. 'It – it – needs some work. It's not – you'll find my music very different from that.'

Anybody's music would have been different from that, I was thinking. But I didn't say anything. I was just glad it was over. So was Beccs. So was Geoffrey Fryer. And Ben. Only Kirsten, and the boys up the back, enjoyed it.

'Did we look all right, though?' Kirsty smiled at Ben, desperate for some words of encouragement from him. 'We can work on the sound,' she said, 'as long as we look all right, can't we?'

Ben stammered, looking at me. 'Well – we – we'd better hear what your – what Amy's going to do. What are you going to do, Amy?'

'Yeah,' the Grunge were calling. They started to clap and chant: 'A-me! A-me! A-me! A-me!'

'I don't know any songs,' I started to say.

'She doesn't know any songs,' Kirsten said over me.

'Except –' I said.

'Sing that one you do,' Beccs surfaced and said. 'Do that old one you do.'

'She does an old one,' Kirsten announced, loud enough to be speaking directly to the boys at the back of the hall.

'Old-one! Old-one! Old-one!' they started to chant.

'Let's hear it, then,' said Ben, indicating that the stage was all mine.

I didn't want to do it. I told them I didn't want to do it; but they said I had to now. They all agreed. Even smiling Stevens agreed from the back of the hall as he wrung his hands and licked his lips in anticipation.

I licked my lips as I ascended the few steps to the stage. My mouth had completely dried up on me. It didn't matter, as I wasn't going to be able to sing at all. I couldn't breathe properly. My feet wouldn't move one in front of the other. Some silly idea of purposely falling down the few stairs and breaking my ankle flitted across my mind; but I wouldn't be able to stand the laughter from the back of the hall. It was bad enough as it was. I had to turn to face it, with Beccs unable to look at me, as I was unable to watch her, but with Kirsten smirking by her side. Some of Kirsten's hair had been flipped and had fallen onto Ben's shoulder. She was smirking as if she knew where her hair had fallen, as if it was going to affect my singing and bring it down to a level even lower than her own.

It was her face that changed my mind, nothing to do with Ben Lyons. Kirsten's face challenged me to sing my old song like another survivor. I felt a sudden rush of angry strength that gave me the breath I needed to start to sing:

You would seize the day for me,
Keep the night away for me,
Make the darkness light for me,
The noble sun ignite for me,
If ever, if ever you were here.

And if ever you were here again
I'd never shed a tear again
Or make the sunrise mine alone
Or see a new sun shine alone
If ever, if ever you were here.

But nothing is forever now I know
The sunrise and the day will go,
As the sun will burn to death one day
To be with you where you have gone,
Where suns and stars have never shone . . .

. . . all the way through.

I went at it as if I was on my own, or trying to quieten my sisters in the morning with my mum grizzling over the sink. My voice increased in strength and confidence as I went through the old lyrics that I knew so well. I filled the school hall with my sound. I could do it. I could feel the size and emptiness of the hall and I could bring out sound enough to fill every square centimetre. At one point, some kind of mathematical construction passed through my mind, as if I was working out, calculating how much sound would be necessary to pack this place properly. I worked it out. The grunge up the back, and Geoffrey Fryer, showed their silenced, blinking faces, as did my friend Beccs, at last, while her cousin's long hair flopped from Ben's shoulder. Only Ben's face showed nothing at all. Absolutely nothing.

I worked the song through to the end, controlling my

voice, keeping it pitch-perfect, loud enough to fill all the available space and no louder. It sounded different here, with so much more room to let it loose, with an audience, however small and local, however hostile.

The silence at the end of the song seemed to have a sound all of its own. I could hear a reverberating disturbance in the metal rafters of the roof, in the open stage curtains that were still, but only just, as if a breeze had just blown through.

Nobody said anything. Even the two leftover grungsters at the back kept as quiet as the curtains. I looked down at Ben. He was looking up at me.

'Now scream,' he said.

'Scream?' I said.

'Scream.'

I looked over at Stevens and Bradshaw. They were still silent. They were waiting. Beccs and Kirsty were waiting, with the face of a friend and an enemy. Geoffrey Fryer was waiting, as if he was afraid of the thing he waited for.

Ben waited.

I screamed. I felt all the little hairs on the back of my neck stand up. I felt Ben feeling the same. I felt Ben feeling like I did.

***Four**

I screamed. The scream stayed with me all the way home, running through my head until my mother's scream of frustration took its place.

'Where have you been?' she shouted, over the twinned chorus of my twin sisters' crying. 'These two have been driving me mad. You're not here, your father's not here!'

'I told you I was going to be late.'

'I know! I know! I didn't think it would be so – anyway, your father! It's about time – I have to do it all!'

'There's a new boy at school!' I shouted.

The twins were having a screaming contest. They bounced off each other, the two so-similar little girls. Sometimes they were both miserable, sometimes both happy. If they were miserable they screamed at each other. Happy, they screamed together, for fun. They often pulled each other's hair to make the fun all the louder. Now one of them was pulling all the stuff out of the low cupboards in the kitchen, while the other one created a diversion by eating the coconut mat just inside the back door. They both had ears full of mashed chips.

'I wish I was at school,' my mum said, trying to clean the grit from Joanna's gums. I had to go and rescue Georgina from the bottles of bleach and the cleaning fluids and floor cloths. 'I'd give anything,' my mum said. 'Absolutely anything.'

She was supposed to have gone to her wine club this

evening. My father must have gone instead, only he'd be tasting his in some bar or pub somewhere. It happened on Friday nights, often, too often. My mum never really knew. She'd usually have left by the time he was home, to her wine club; which, in reality, was just a chance to sit and have a drink and a chat to some old school colleagues of hers. She'd been a secondary school teacher up until just a couple of months or so before the twins were born. That's what she was, a secondary school teacher, tough talking, clever and quick. She knew what she wanted and how to get people to do it. One day, she'd be head of some school somewhere. That was what she wanted, eventually. It should have happened years ago, but she enjoyed the actual face-to-face teaching too much. She was simply too good at it.

Now, though, look what had happened to her. She tried to study yoga and acupuncture, to pin herself down to some kind of relaxed and healthy state. The stress of teaching a whole class full of secondary school kids was nothing compared to trying to keep control of two sicky pre-playschool babies. She was coming to bits at the seams. She felt deserted, as if the twins were her fault.

'As if somebody has to be to blame for them,' she'd often said to me, trying not to shed another tear. 'I'm not to blame,' she'd say, 'am I?'

She was dying of being cooped up, with no stimulation for her mind other than deciding which twin stank worse, so needed changing first. 'I'm an intellectual woman,' she'd say, so often. 'I don't need this, at my time of life.'

'Neither do I,' my dad would say, on his way out. He worked harder and longer than he ever had in his life. He got out of the house. He came back late, especially on a Friday night. My mother never knew how late though, as she'd be tasting wine herself and I'd be there on my own with my sisters until my father decided to roll in with a red wine stain on his top lip and cigar ash over the baby-stains on his blue pinstriped suit.

I screamed. The twins screamed. My mum screamed. Our whole house was a single scream sometimes. That's why the neighbours looked at us as they did. We had no right having these babies we could not handle. Even the old lady next door disapproved of my mother's late pregnancy. I looked more like the twins' auntie than their sister. A girl that lived just down the way, my age, already had a baby of her own. Imagine that; a baby with a couple of aunties that were babies themselves.

When I told Beccs my mum was pregnant, she said: 'Ugh!'

We laughed, because it was funny. Only it wasn't really. When Kirsten heard about it and laughed and called it tacky, it wasn't funny at all. But I had to laugh. I had to. I had to make it as funny as I could, or else it would have to be as un-funny as it was.

As unfunny as now, with my dad missing until late on a Friday night and my mum too close to tears again. I wanted to tell her what I'd been doing, why I was late.

'There's a new boy at school!' I hollered.

'I wish I was at school,' she simpered, adding to her wish list as she went along. It was far too long as it was, my mother's wish list.

We were wrestling a baby each at the time. My sisters were big, bonny kids, with a set of vocal chords each to match my own. 'Sing your song!' my mother cried. 'Sing your song and shut them up for a minute.'

'I've been singing my song,' I said.

'Sing it again then! Sing anything!'

'I'll show them my maths, shall I?' I shouted, because I

needed to show *someone* my maths. We were a fair way though the first term of Year Twelve and I was already going from good to not so good, to bad. From there, where I seemed to be, I could see worse looming, then worse still. I needed help. No, I needed my mum's help. She had always given me my pictures of understanding. She had always understood me, and the difficulties I'd be most likely to have in understanding anything. She had always given me a path, a route plan through my nervous confusion to a simplified solution. She used to be a clever, clever teacher, a working mother, but with the time and the patience to steer me clear.

'Sing anything!' she hollered now, as one or the other of my similar sisters popped with sick over her again. 'Sing them a nursery rhyme. A sea shanty. Verdi's *Requiem*. Anything.'

So I sang Humpty Dumpty, Kings, Horses and Men to Georgie and Jo in their cots as my mother changed her clothes. She had been ready to go out, until she was puked and put upon, screamed at to go and change back into her old skirt and top.

The twins were dropping off to sleep. I could hear my mother trying to breathe as she cricked herself into an uncomfortable yoga position in her bedroom. A year or so ago, she'd never have bothered with yoga or reiki or any of the other wonderful self-control or energy concentrating remedies she was into. She'd changed so much, so quickly. She had, so had my dad. So had I.

I knocked softly on her bedroom door. She quietly called me in, locked as she was in a painful lotus. 'I think my knees have gone,' she said, reaching out for me. I had to help untangle her, straightening her limbs as one after the other her knees gave a very nasty crack. 'You need to practise this stuff,' she said, wincing. 'It takes time. You have to have so much time to practise, you shouldn't need it in the first place.

39

If I had enough time to practise relaxing, I wouldn't be so tense, would I?'

'No, Mum,' I said, giving her a hug. It used to be that she gave hugs to me. Not now though, not now. 'I need some help, Mum,' I said. 'With my maths.'

She looked up at me with a kind of half confused expression on her face, as if she was trying to remember what was meant by the word maths. All her former personality and intelligence had been sidelined, put away somewhere in storage. I watched her trying to collect herself, or what was left of herself. 'I'm sorry,' she said, 'of course. Amy, I'm sorry.'

'Mum, don't. I'll get my books, shall I?'

'Yes, you get your books. Bring them back in here. We'll sit on the bed together, yes?'

'Yes,' I said. We could have sat on the bed too, working through my maths problems together, quite simply, quite without a fuss. If one or the other then both twins hadn't started up as I was on my way back to my mum's bedroom, we would have done that. As it was, my mum came tearing past me on the landing with that look of long, long suffering back on her face. I halted for only a moment before turning back to my own room.

I put on some dance music and sat at my table blinking into my textbook. There was an explanation in front of my nose that described the differential coefficients of sine x and cosine x.

If $y = \sin x$, $\dfrac{dy}{dx} = \cos x$.

If $y = \cos x$, $\dfrac{dy}{dx} = -\sin x$.

Why? How?

I could have looked at that little lot for a million years. I had looked at it for a million years. The time of my lack of understanding ticked heavily, as if I was just waiting to fail, or for my execution. I'd tried asking my teacher, Mr Rosenthal. He'd worked through it and worked through it so many times I felt embarrassed to ask again; so didn't ask. But got no pictures. I was entirely outside of this. It was beyond me. It was in one place, I was in another.

The trouble was, it was affecting all my studies. The physics were also running away from me. Biology wasn't so bad, but seemed almost pointless now, without the other two to back it up.

Mr Rosenthal was a nice man. He was a teacher; he should have been able to help me understand. But he wasn't *that* good a teacher. I needed something more, something special. I needed my mother. But she was more like another Mr Rosenthal when she finally caught up with me at my little writing desk in my room. She came in with one ear still cocked for the slightest whimper from one baby or the other, looking over my shoulder at the problem I was struggling with.

I glanced from my desk light at her darkened features. 'I don't get this,' I said.

She looked at the open pages. 'Differential coefficient of sine x and cosine x,' she stated. 'What don't you understand?'

'Any of it,' I said. 'I just don't get it.'

'No,' she said, looking away from the light.

I had to sit there waiting while her mind wandered. 'Mum?' I said, eventually. 'I need help with this.'

'Yes,' she said, her attention snapping back to the open pages. 'Yes, look, look at it like this. It's easier to draw the sine wave then by a series of tangents plot its rate of change. You'll see at its maximum its rate of change is in fact

41

nil, and at the zero point its rate of change is at maximum. If you plot that, it's easy to see how you'll get a cosine wave. See?'

'No,' I said. 'I can't see.'

'Look,' she said, 'find me a pencil and a piece of paper. Look,' she said, starting to draw the curves she needed to make a picture-explanation for me. 'Look, that's a –'

Then the front door slammed. It slammed through the house, informing us all that my father had come home. The twins were informed of the fact, starting up again in a unison welcome wail for the return of their daddy.

The pencil fell from my mother's hand onto the paper and she was immediately at the top of the stairs yelling: 'Can't you slam the door any louder!'

To which a yell returned: 'Of course I can!' and the door was opened again and slammed all the louder.

'That's it!' my mother shouted. 'You wake them up, go on! I've only just got them both to sleep, and you come in and immediately wake them up!'

'And hello to you too, darling!' he shouted up the stairs. Another door slammed downstairs.

My mother's feet were thundering down, the door opening again. 'What's the matter with you?' she was shouting at him.

'Well what's the matter with you, then?' he was shouting back. 'At least let me get through the door.'

I was left blinking down at the two curves my mother had drawn on the blank sheet in front of me.

'You were through the door!' came my mother's voice next. 'Anyone can hear that! What time do you call this?'

'I call it the time it is,' my father's voice came. 'What time do *you* call it?'

'I call it late. Where've you been?'

'I haven't been anywhere, have I. I can't go anywhere. Where can I go?'

'Well you manage to go somewhere nearly every evening, don't you?'

'I'm working, aren't I.'

'Are you? Until this time?'

'It's Friday. You go out on Fridays, don't you? You go out nearly every night!'

'Do I? I try to, but how can I go out when you never turn up till this late?'

'Amy was here, wasn't she?'

'Was she? What makes you think so?'

'She's always here, isn't she?'

'Always? You always this late then, are you?'

'Is that what she said?'

'No!'

'Have you asked her?'

'No. But I might.'

'Go on then! Go on! Ask her! Go on!'

I looked down at the sheet of paper in front of me. The picture was incomplete. This was just about as far as my mother ever got.

I thought back to the singing we did after school. I remembered my scream. The world seemed full of screams, listening to my parents and to my baby sisters. Of all the screams in the world, only mine felt good. It had felt very good.

I was going to have to scream a whole lot more.

★★★ Five

'**W**hat *is* she wearing?' I asked Beccs.

Kirsten was done up in some hot-pants outfit with the sleeves of her jacket and her shorts rolled. She had on boots, DMs, with black socks peeping over the tops.

'What?' said Beccs. 'She looks all right. Leave her alone.'

Becca had on the short skirt I'd seen her wearing in town the other Saturday. But now she was wearing a new top too, which was too tight for her and showed off too much fat.

'I think Kirsty looks really good,' she said, loud enough for her cousin to hear.

'I think Becky looks cool, too,' said Kirsten, looking me slowly up and down as if I'd just trodden in dog's muck.

We were meeting up to go over to Geoffrey Fryer's place. His parents had a big house, with this kind of out-house or granny-annexe we could use. The Grunge Machine had tried to rehearse there once, he'd told us, but there hadn't been enough room for Peter Stevens' drum kit plus all the other amplifiers and speakers and long leads. All the indie paraphernalia filled the place and left them no room to play anything. 'That's w-why we were-weren't very good,' Geoff told us.

We had nodded, glancing at each other.

'Is that why?' Ben said.

Geoffrey nodded nervously, smiled. He stopped smiling. He laughed. 'It didn't h-help,' he said, 'cause n-none of us c-could – could play.'

44

'You can, Geoff,' Ben said. 'You just need the right stuff to play. You wait and see on Sunday.'

So on Sunday we were on our way to Geoff's house, with Kirsten looking like a pair of legs on legs and Rebecca like a Scotsman in too short a kilt. You could tell, at a glance, that we were off to meet Ben Fryer. Kirsten and Rebecca had it written all over them.

Me? I was wearing my jeans and trainers as usual, with a stripy tee shirt I'd stumbled across while hiding from Beccs in the mall the other day. I looked all right. You know, a little on the short side, a little boyish perhaps, but this was me. I looked how I looked. No make-up, either. Not like Kirsten's 'Becky-girl'. Especially not like Kirsten, whose face was all made-over and plastercasted like a ceramic doll. She pouted and preened until we arrived at Geoffrey's and found Ben hadn't arrived yet.

Geoff's mum showed us into the little flat where at least he was waiting for us. Geoff's mum was long and slender, but with a bend from the waist to the left as if she was always veering round a corner. His dad, Ben had told us the other day, was a builder, or rather a demolisher with his own decon-struction business, a huge bloke who knocked houses over with his bare head. Geoffrey, evidently, took after his mum. 'Here they are, my Geoffrey,' she said, as we swept into the apartment behind her, 'here's all your little friends.'

Geoffrey was blushing at Kirsten as his mum said that. Kirsten's hair was flying; she looked at me as if to accuse me of being a little friend, as that description certainly didn't fit her.

'Hello, Geoff,' I said, happy to be friendly, if not quite so satisfied with being quite this little.

'Where's Ben?' Kirsty said, as soon as Geoff's mum was out of the room.

'He's n-not here yet,' Geoff said.

'So you can stop posing for five minutes,' I went and said, before I could stop myself.

'I suppose it must look like that to you,' she said, turning on me, 'from right down there.'

'Leave it out, you two,' Beccs said. 'Geoff, this place – it's really good.'

'Is it?' Geoff said, looking round, unsure of where he was.

'Yeah,' Beccs said. 'It's like having a place of your own.'

'It's somewhere to go,' I said, 'to be on your own for a while.'

'Yeah,' Geoff said, 'b-but my mum k-keeps –'

'Anyone like some pop?' Geoff's mum popped up that very moment and said, holding up a carrier bag full of cans of cherry coke and lemonade.

Geoffrey nearly folded in half with supreme embarrassment in front of Kirsten.

'Yes, thanks very much Mrs Fryer,' I said, taking the bag from her. 'That'll be very nice, thank you.'

'Ooh,' she wafted, gazing down on me like a giraffe, 'aren't you a sweet one? Geoffrey, what's this sweet one called?'

'I'm Amy,' I said, as Geoff cringed closed, clenched into a kind of zigzag pattern.

'She's called Amy Peppercorn,' lovely Kirsten had to go and say.

'Is she?' Mrs Fryer sang in delight. 'Amy Peppercorn? What a lovely name.'

'Isn't it,' Kirsten pretended to sweet-tooth with her.

'And what's your name?' Mrs Fryer asked.

'I'm Kirsty. And this is my cousin, Becky.'

'All such lovely names,' Mrs Fryer gushed. 'Aren't they all lovely names, Geoffrey?'

Poor Geoff was almost spiral shaped by this time; he looked

like a model of his own DNA strands, he was so wrenched. He was red raw.

'And aren't you a lovely one,' Mrs Fryer said, as Kirsten preened and pouted in front of her. 'Geoffrey, isn't she a –'

'Actually,' I found myself suddenly saying, 'Becky's called Beccs. She plays a lot of football, don't you Beccs?'

Mrs Fryer tried to look at her as if she thought playing football was nice. 'That's nice, dear,' she said.

'Yeah,' Beccs said, 'I play football better than Geoff plays keyboards, isn't that right Geoff?'

'Yeah,' Geoff managed to say, uncurling slightly.

'He needs a bit of practice, our Geoffrey,' Beccs said. 'Don't you Geoffrey?'

Geoff nodded.

His mum gave Beccs a brief, tight smile. 'Well,' she said, 'I'd better let you get on and practise, then, hadn't I?'

'Thanks for the pop, Mrs Fryer,' I said, holding up the carrier.

'Your mum's really nice,' Kirsten said, as soon as she'd veered out of the door of the granny flat.

Geoff cringed again, but managed a little smile of gratitude towards Beccs and me. Beccs never knew how good she was at getting people out of situations. She never knew how good she was at handling people. But I suppose she had to be, with Kirsten and me round her all the time, continually making situations that she had to try to handle.

Like now, for example, with us all getting out our copies of Ben's song over our cans of Mrs Fryer's 'pop', with Kirsten insisting that she was the only one capable of reading.

The song was called 'Hell To Pay'. Kirsten didn't like it, because it was all about cars and crashes and trouble. The band was going to be called Car Crime, which was a whole lot better than Grunge Machine, but, in Kirsten's opinion, didn't seem right for a band with a boy on the keyboards and one on the drum machine, but fronted by three cute girl singers. 'You don't understand,' she was trying to tell us, 'you don't get it. It's like stealing cars or something.'

'The band's called Car Crime,' I said.

'It's a c-c-cool n-name,' Geoff said.

'You think so?' Kirsten snapped at him, drying him to a crisp once again. 'Car Crime? We should be called – I think we should be called Girl Friday, or something.'

'Girl Friday?' I gagged. 'Girl Friday?'

'It's a good name,' she said. 'Becky likes it, don't you Becky?'

'Oh,' I said, 'so you've been discussing it, have you?'

'I never said I liked it or not,' Beccs had to say, trying to handle the situation again. 'I just said Car Crime sounds more like a boy band than something with three girl singers.'

'We haven't sung anything yet,' I said.

'Except old songs,' Kirsten said, with a tight little smile in my direction.

'And wannabe copies of girl groups,' I said.

'B-but –' Geoffrey was continuously trying to say, but managing to get nothing past our worsening bicker and his own stutter.

'And I don't get all these lyrics,' Beccs said. 'There's so many –'

'It's about some kind of car crime,' Kirsten said.

'Oh, really?' I went. 'Is that a fact?'

'If you read between the lines,' Kirsten started to say.

'I was being ironic,' I said. 'If you know what irony is?'

'No,' Beccs said, 'I just meant so many words to fit in. It goes on and on.'

48

'B-but –' Geoff said.

'I know what irony is,' Kirsten said. 'Do you know what sarcasm is?'

'It's a rap,' I said.

'What, sarcasm?'

'No. The lyric. Some kind of rap. Look at it.'

'I'm not rapping,' Kirsten said. 'I didn't know this was going to be a rap band.'

'Everyone's doing rap,' Beccs said.

'B-but –' said Geoffrey.

'Rap's rubbish,' Kirsten said.

'What do you know about rap?' I said.

'What is there to know?' she said.

'Beccs likes rap,' I said. 'Don't you?'

'B-but –' Geoff said.

'It's all the same, isn't it?' Kirsten said.

'No,' Beccs said.

'N-no –' said Geoff.

'No?' I said.

'No?' from Kirsten.

'N-no!' stammered Geoff.

'No, I –' stammered Beccs, 'Yes, I – some rap's good. No, it's not all the same. Some's all right.'

'No!' said Geoffrey, too deliberately.

We looked at him, Kirsten, Beccs and me. We were all getting angry and frustrated. How were we ever going to find music that we'd all enjoy and want to be a part of? Even Geoff was saying no forcefully enough to make us all stop and look at him.

'I-it's – B-Ben's,' he said. He looked down, unable to face us for long; then he looked back up: 'Ben's band,' he said. 'N-not yours.'

'Well I never said it was mine,' said Kirsten, as if Geoff had been speaking directly to her alone. 'I just thought Girl Friday was a good name for a band with three girl singers.'

Geoff was shaking his head. 'C-car C-c –'

'Crime,' Ben's voice said from behind us. 'Car Crime is what the band's called, people,' he said, coming in, helping himself to a can of drink. 'Your mum let me come through, Geoff.'

'Hi, Ben,' Kirsten called.

'Hi,' he said. 'How we all doing?'

'We're doing fine,' Beccs said, smiling now, like Kirsten, as Ben opened his can of cherry cola.

'We were all just wondering,' I said, 'what kind of music we're going to be playing?'

'Playing?' Kirsten said. 'Who's playing anything?'

'We don't know,' Beccs said, 'if this song's rap or – something – or what.'

Ben smiled. Kirsty and Becky smiled too. 'Like your tee shirt,' he said, looking at me. Funnily enough, he was wearing one quite like it. And jeans, like mine. And trainers, too.

'You two could be brothers,' Kirsten said.

Ben laughed. I don't think he found it funny, but he laughed anyway. He was looking at me, I think. I'm not sure, because for some reason I was feeling kind of too hot all of a sudden, flushed, kind of thing, a little bit dizzy. Even that last caustic comment from Kirsty went sailing straight over my head with practically no effect. Ben was looking at me. So was Beccs. I could feel myself getting hot.

'Rap?' Ben said, suddenly. 'Rap? R and B? Hip hop? Dance? Old School? Indie? Rock? Punk? What the hell does all that mean? Forget it. We're going to do our music, that's what we're going to do. Isn't that right, Geoff?'

Geoff nodded and nodded, as if his nodding head stuttered too.

'See?' Ben said. 'You just gotta hear some of the stuff Geoff can do. This fella's good, I'm telling you.'

We were all looking at Geoffrey now, as he screwed himself into a ball. I hadn't realised that putting a band together was going to be so embarrassing. We were all going to put ourselves on the spot, leaving ourselves, each of us, wide open to ridicule. I wondered for a minute why we were doing it.

Then I looked at Kirsty, the way she was looking at Ben; I could see why she was doing this. I looked at Beccs in her new mini-skirt; she was staring at Ben. And if Geoff really could play those keyboards, that, I supposed, was enough of a reason for him. But what was I doing here? And why was Ben here, with us, like this?

'Why are we doing this in the first place?' I suddenly found myself asking Ben. The others looked at me quite shocked, as if I'd said something really stupid or insulting to Ben personally.

He smiled. 'Listen,' he said. He went over to the equipment he and Geoff had already piled against the wall. Geoff was behind his keyboards. Ben switched everything on. There was a rich low humming sound that filled the background of the room. There was a buzz of expectation just out of earshot, an excitement that cut through me, tingling up my spine to the roots of my hair.

'Feel that?' said Ben.

'Feel what?' said Kirsty.

Ben looked at me. I tingled as if my hair was all standing on end. 'That's what I'm doing here,' he said. 'And that's why you're here too.'

I glanced at Beccs. She was looking at Ben, at me, at Ben.

Ben nodded to Geoff: 'Ready?' he said. Geoffrey stuttered out his manic nod.

'Good,' Ben said, turning to me. 'Now scream.'

 # Six

'Lost your job? What do you mean, lost your job?' That was my mum, Jill, screaming at Tony, my dad. I'd been screaming for weeks, with Car Crime, with Ben Lyons. I screamed there, with the band. Here: 'What do you mean, lost your job?'

'What do you think I mean? How many meanings are there when somebody says, I lost my job? I lost my job is what I mean. That's exactly what I mean, nothing else. Do you get it? I lost my job!'

They were glaring at each other. My mother's mouth was twitching, searching for something to say next. She was blinking at a phenomenal rate, like a ham actor in a silent film wishing to portray disbelief. 'I don't believe it,' she said, when her mouth finally found the words. 'I do not believe it.'

'Why not?' my father shrugged, as if telling us this was an everyday occurrence, 'what's to disbelieve?'

We were all bunched in the kitchen on the morning I'd been waiting weeks for, weeks of rehearsals and arrangements, insincere flattery, ego massaging and levelling of heads. You wouldn't believe what I'd been through trying to get Car Crime's first gig off the ground in our school hall this evening: three quarters of an hour of being pilloried by classmates and class-enemies alike. I'd been through it all, for this.

And now: 'I don't believe it,' my mother was gasping. 'I do not believe it.'

'Why not?' my father actually shrugged. 'What's to disbelieve?'

The twins were silent for once, both blinking like their mother. They couldn't believe what they were hearing, either. I could though. I'd found it easy to believe, when he'd told me about it the day before.

'Can you believe this?' my mother turned and said to me.

The twins were shaking their heads. No, they couldn't believe it at all. My head was going down, keeping well out of the way. I'd told my dad that he had to tell my mum he hadn't actually been working for the past two weeks.

'What happened?' she said, my mother, with her face still turned in my direction.

I was going to deny all knowledge, tell her that it was nothing to do with me. They'd have to sort it out themselves.

But: 'What happened?' she shrieked, turning back to look at him.

'I told them where to stick it, didn't I! What else could have happened? There was no end to it. Whatever I did, whatever I contributed, they wanted more. I couldn't stand it.'

'So you just told them to stick it, did you? Oh, good idea.'

'I had to.'

'Of course you did! Of course you did!'

I was watching the twins, how very quiet they'd become. They were intent on watching their parents, both with a twinned line of dribble hanging from their nearly identical chins.

'Of course you did! Tell them where to stick their job! That's the way to get a reference, isn't it? That's how to get a reference for another job, isn't it?'

'I don't care! I –'

'No? Don't care then! Neither do I! In fact, I'm glad. I'm very glad, because you'll be the one stuck at home looking after these poor little mites, won't you!'

I glanced up to see the horror in my dad's face as he looked at the poor little mites in their tomato-ketchup high chairs and their dangerous nappies and dribbly chins.

'Yes!' my mother started smiling, but cruelly. 'That's made up my mind for me. I'm going back to work.'

'No!' my dad snapped. The twins jumped in their chairs. 'No you're not!'

'No?' my mum said defiantly. The twins shook their heads in stunning simultaneity.

'Well who's going to make the money then, eh? Who? You? Amy? Eh?'

'See!' my dad called over at me. 'See?'

I ducked, but too late.

'I told you she'd be like this. I told you!'

My mum glared over at me. The twins, in full dribble, gazed at me, fascinated by all the noise they were not having to make.

'What do you mean: I told you?' she said, glaring at my dad, back at me. 'Did you know about this, Amy? Did you tell her about this?' she snapped back at my dad.

His cheeks were aglow, ruddy and hot, as if painted. He looked like a cartoon, or more like a puppet, Mr Peppercorn on strings with stuck open eyes in his beetroot complexion. 'I told you she'd be like this,' he said again. 'She thinks I can't get another job.'

'When did you tell her?' she said, turning to me. 'When did he tell you?'

'Last night!' he snapped. 'I had to tell someone.'

'So you decided to burden your daughter instead of me. Is that it? And why are you dressed for work? You've been dressing for work every morning, haven't you? How long's it been?'

'A week,' he said, glancing at me.

'A week?'

'Two weeks.'

'Two weeks! Two weeks since you've been to work? You've been lying to me – you've been lying to all of us.'

'I wanted to – I wanted to find another job.'

'And have you?'

'Not yet. I will though. I will.'

'Yes? When? How long can we go on without money, do you think?'

'I'm being paid until the end of the month.'

'Oh. A week and a bit, then. Well you'd better go and find a job, hadn't you.'

'I will.'

'Go on, then!'

'Mum,' I said.

'Go on, then!' she yelled at him.

'Mum,' I said again.

'Go on!' she screamed. 'If you think it's easy to get jobs with no references! Go on! Go on! See what you can do!'

'All right!' he screamed back, his arm flailing, accidentally knocking a teacup smashing to the kitchen floor.

'That's right!' screamed my mother. 'Smash the house up now, why don't you?'

'All right then!' he screamed, picking up another cup and dashing it to the floor. 'All right, I will then!'

'Dad!' I screamed. 'Mum! Stop it! Stop it now, both of you! What's the matter with you?'

They stopped. The place went silent. The fragmented cups lay still, cups no longer, their dregs of wasted tea simply more stains on the baby-stained kitchen floor.

As if at a predetermined moment, the twins burst into screaming wails of dissatisfaction at all the renewed silence they had battled so hard against.

'Now look what you've done!' my mother shouted above the screams at my father.

'I haven't done that!' he wailed back. 'They're your responsibility, not mine.'

'Oh!' she shouted. 'I knew it! I knew it was all my fault! I knew you were going to blame me for everything!'

'Mum!' I shouted.

The twins screamed louder; the louder they screamed, the louder my dad shouted. 'I'm not going to – to hell with all this!' he shouted, swinging the door open, slamming it closed behind him. The front door slammed even harder a second or two after that.

'Shut them up!' my mum called to me. 'Please, Amy, do something.' She was in tears.

'I have to go, Mum. I'll be late for school.'

'How about if I write you a note? No – you're right. You must go to school. It's the most important thing. You go. Have you taken your tablets? We don't want you –'

I picked Georgina out of her chair. 'Get Jo,' I said.

'No,' she said, taking Georgie from me. 'You have to go to school. I'm sorry. You mustn't miss school and fall behind. Your studies are the most important thing at the moment. You go. Go and do well at school for me.'

She was crying. She made me feel so old, so sensibly mature in comparison to the tears she could shed. My father had the same effect on me, coming quietly into my bedroom to confess that he'd lost his job because he couldn't stand it. He should never have taken the job in the first place. It had been wrong for him. But he explained all this to me, in secret, whispering to me as I lay awake last night with Ben and the band on my mind and my maths books slung under the bed. He told me all this, when he should have been telling my mother. I had maths problems of my own.

'You'll have to tell Mum,' I told him.

'That's not an easy thing to do,' he said.

'Neither is my maths,' I said.

He laughed, quietly. 'You'll have to get your mother's help with that. You know how useless I am at explaining maths. Ask your mum.'

I had tried to ask her, just as my father must have tried to tell her about his job and how useless he was at it.

The twins were screaming, trying to bring down the house as my mother told me, in tears, to go and do well at school. I said I would, but knew I would not. I was telling lies, like my father, for the same reasons as he had. Everything was going wrong, but we all had to speak and behave as if everything was fine. My mother's tears of frustration wouldn't allow the truth to enter this house without shattered cups and far, far more screams.

I felt old and tired as I left the house. The twins seemed so worldly and wise, screaming the house down before, during and after everything went wrong. Of the whole household, only I wasn't allowed to scream.

'You'll be home on time, tonight,' my mother had told, rather than asked me.

'Mum, we're doing the – I'm singing tonight, I told you. Remember?'

My mother's shoulders had sunk. 'That's me in for another evening, I suppose. Because I don't know what time he'll decide to show his face again. When he fancies it, I expect. I don't really think that's fair. Do you think that's at all fair?'

My shoulders sank.

'Oh,' she said, 'but you get off to school. You've got enough to worry about, doing your thing with that band of yours, having fun. You go. I'll be all right.'

I went. She was right; I did have enough to worry about. She was crying. The twins were screaming. Everyone in that house was allowed to scream – everyone but me. Of them all, I had to be silent, to sing when I was told, to go to school and do well. Well I wasn't doing well at school. Yes, I was doing my thing with that band of mine, or Ben's; but I wasn't singing. I was screaming.

My father was waiting for me down the road a little way, hidden round the first bend. I couldn't get away that easily. 'I told you,' he told me, 'that it'd be like that. She doesn't want to listen. I don't think that's fair, do you?'

My shoulders sank. 'Dad,' I said, 'I've just got to go to school.'

'Yes,' he said, 'yes, of course. You've got enough with your own worries, haven't you? You don't want me burdening you with mine, I understand.'

'Dad. It isn't – look, just – go and look for a job, but be home early this afternoon. Mum wants to go to her yoga class, or whatever she does tonight.'

'I know,' he said, walking by my side with his hands in his business suit pockets, 'I can never remember either. All that stuff she does. I don't know why she does it.'

'Don't you?' I said, genuinely surprised. What was I supposed to do, explain it to him? They were supposed to be the adults, not me. I couldn't work it out for them. What did they expect of me?

'No,' he said, 'I don't. What does she think she's going to

get out of it? Acupuncture? What's she want to go round sticking things in people for?'

'I don't think she even does acupuncture, does she?'

'Doesn't she?'

'I don't know. Anyway,' I said, 'wouldn't you like to stick a few pins in people, sometimes?'

'Yes,' he said, 'but not to make them feel better. Quite the reverse, in fact.'

'Just be home early tonight, Dad,' I said. 'Please.'

'Won't you be there, then?'

'No, I – we're doing that thing tonight, with the band, at school, you know?'

'Ah,' he said, 'your gig. That's what you call it, a gig, isn't it?'

I hated it when my dad said things like that. Like sometimes when he tried to listen to my music. Or if we were watching TV and something with sex came on, and he'd try to act all cool about it, but end up making the embarrassment much, much worse for everybody.

My mum didn't used to do stuff like that. She accepted the fact that she was of her generation and I was of mine. That was a much better way. Except that she went and got pregnant and did away with all the trust I had in her. She turned out to be as bad as he was, with her morning sickness and her cravings for weird food and her walking about outside in the street in broad daylight where all my friends and their dead uncool parents would see her and speak to her and know all about our horrid little lives.

Now my dad walked with me towards my school, wanting to talk to me about gigs and about the problems he was having with his career and his relationships. I could see Kirsty and Beccs walking just a little way up ahead without their dads or their mums or their tiny sisters' screams still ringing in their ears. 'Dad,' I had to say, 'just go and look for a job and go home early and help Mum with the twins today, okay?'

'Of course I will,' he said. 'That's what I was going to do. Hey, aren't those your friends up there?'

'Yes, Dad. See you tonight.'

'Hi, girls.'

'Hello, Mr Peppercorn,' they said, Kirsty and Beccs. They sounded like something from a kids' cartoon. Mr Peppercorn Goes To School, tra-la-la, la-la.

'See you tonight, Dad,' I said, sighing.

'Yes. See you tonight,' he said, kissing me, walking away. But then he turned. 'Oh,' he said, 'good luck with the concert tonight, girls.'

Kirsty and Beccs smiled and waved. My dad waved back at them. He looked so buoyant and happy, I could hardly believe it was the same person I'd watched breaking cups in the kitchen only twenty minutes earlier.

'Concert?' Beccs said.

'I know,' I said, grimacing. 'Dads, eh?'

'I think he's really sweet, your dad,' Kirsty said.

'He's not like my old man, anyway,' said Beccs. 'My old fella's just so embarrassing, you wouldn't believe it.'

'Yeah?' I said. ' "Good luck with the concert"? How embarrassing's that?'

'Anyway,' Kirsten said, 'it doesn't matter, because we're probably not doing anything, not now.'

'Now?' I said. 'Why?'

'Oh,' Kirsten said, 'Geoff's not doing it because of Peter Stevens.'

'Stevens and Michael Bradshaw are going to beat Geoff up,' Beccs said.

'But Geoff's too much of a little girl,' Kirsten said, 'to do anything about it.'

★*★

We'd been through so much embarrassment, just to get it to this stage, I wasn't going to let Stevens and the rest of that grunge stop us. I wanted this now, because I'd already put so much into it. The whole thing was only just hanging together as it was, and we were supposed to be doing this 'concert', as my dad called it, in the school hall tonight.

The thing is, I couldn't seem to concentrate on anything but Ben – anything but the band. I couldn't think of anything but Ben and the band. My studies were grinding to a halt. I still couldn't get to grips with the differentiation of trigonometrical functions, which was tripping me up with every step I tried to take. It was driving me mad. I couldn't go to my mum with it, because, well, just because. It was because I couldn't have faced her questioning me about my problems, not with Ben so much on my mind. And the band. Not with Ben and the band on my mind all the time.

My mum was so different, too. She didn't even know how I was struggling. At one time, she'd have known. She'd have known everything about me then. Not now.

My dad was too busy being my dad, helpless, struggling with everything he had to do to keep us all. It wasn't their fault. Neither was it mine. I suppose. Or it might have been. I don't know. It's just that everything stacks up, doesn't it? Everything was stacking up against me. My studies, my parents, my friends. You would not believe what I'd had to do to keep everything together with Car Crime.

Kirsten kept complaining that she didn't have enough to do, because I was doing the solo singing and Beccs the rapping and Kirsten was there to – I suppose she was there to dance or something, to do a bit of backing vocals, to look good. She kept making spiteful little remarks about my singing, about the way I looked, my height, the length of my legs, my face, my hair. I had to keep my mouth shut and take it, most of the time. Most of the time. She really got to me. She got to Beccs too, but Beccs couldn't say anything, either.

Sometimes, I couldn't feel that Beccs was my friend at all, really. She was so – she had become so insensitive to the way I was feeling. She didn't see that Kirsty was getting at me, again and again, little by little, wearing me down. She didn't notice how Kirsten was with me, because Kirsty was so good at making Beccs feel good about the way she was changing. And Beccs *was* changing. She was starting to lose weight. She asked Geoff, I overheard one day, to stop calling her Beccs and call her Becky instead. She didn't disagree – at least, I didn't hear her say anything – when Kirsty said the band was going to look pretty stupid with me at the front doing most of the singing. Beccs didn't disagree with her then, or at any other time. Neither did Geoff. But Geoff didn't disagree with anybody, ever. He just looked with doe-eyes at Kirsten as she looked with doe-eyes at Ben. Ben never seemed to notice anything; he was so wrapped up in his music.

We were all wrapped up in Ben's music. It was in my head, for ever. I heard it through the silence of my bedroom when I should have been concentrating on complex differential equations. I was going insane. I couldn't even listen to any of my old CDs; nothing sounded any good any more. Ben was in my head. My pictures were all of him, none of mathematics, physics or biology.

I kept having to go to Ben to tell him Kirsten wasn't happy. I didn't tell him she was driving me mad, that I wasn't happy about losing my best friend to a bimbo, but had to tell him that Kirsten didn't think she was being given enough to do.

'Don't tell her I told you so,' I told him.

'Why not?' Ben said.

'She wouldn't like it,' I said.

So he didn't tell her anything but how good she was looking and how we couldn't do what we wanted to do without her, not properly, anyway. He told her we all had to look the part and without her, well, what were we?

So she was happy with that, looking round at the rest of us as if we all, collectively, amounted to not much more than nothing.

I saw Geoff curling round one cringe after another as Ben said these things to Kirsty, all knotted up inside with jealousy. I saw Beccs's, *Becky's* own hopeless jealousy as she looked down, keeping her eyes to the floor and to herself and definitely away from me. I saw it all, but had to be sure nobody saw me.

I was struggling with my maths, physics, my own biology. I felt things, of course I did; but nothing showed in my expression, nobody noticed me at all.

They were all okay really. Ben and Geoff were studying music, so this project had been written into their studies. Kirsty and Beccs, Becky, were doing English, Art, Business Studies and Physical Education between them. They were feeling jealous, but at least they weren't bombing out on every subject. For them, this band, Car Crime, was just a diversion, a means by which to get closer to Ben. For me – for me, it had become nearly everything.

I couldn't concentrate on anything else. We had a sound. We had a feeling. I felt as Ben felt, I knew I did. He knew it too. He didn't have to say anything to me, to orchestrate me as he and I manipulated the others, playing one against the other, using his charm to work little wonders of motivation and assurance. He had only to look at me. I don't know why I didn't hate it that he had so much power over me. But he and I both knew when something was right, so I stopped questioning it. Ben never questioned me; I never questioned him. We looked at each other every now and then; I had some power too, I hoped: that was enough.

The situation between my parents was deteriorating. The special relationship I'd had with my mother ever since I could remember never recovered from the long pregnancy she suffered. Something fundamental changed in her during those laborious months. Producing two healthy twin girls took too much from her. They had been taking too much ever since. Both she and my father seemed to assume that I was set to do well and to develop automatically, without their help and concentration.

I seemed to have become anonymous in the eyes of my parents, as they struggled to raise their youngest daughters. Their struggle with me was over, or so it seemed. That's how it felt, anyway, to me.

One of my tutors, Mrs McKintyre, had started noticing the changes in me. She had questioned me, trying to find out what was going wrong. My biology results had never been this bad. She was beginning to wonder what was going wrong with me.

I think she thought I might be taking drugs or getting myself in trouble some other way. Well, she might have been right. I was hooked, just not on what she suspected. I had to have my bi-weekly dose of working with the band. We were Car Crime. We were going to do our stuff in the school hall that Friday. Everyone would be expecting dodgy cover versions of chart hits. They looked at Kirsty in her Courtney Schaeffer pop outfits and expected that what we had was built around that. Well it wasn't. It was built around what Ben and I had made together. I could sing Ben's songs. He could write music for me. We told each other so, exchanging looks, time after time.

Now Geoff said, at the very last minute, that he wasn't going on stage because of Stevens and Bradshaw and their grunge gang. I couldn't let that happen. I had invested too much in this. I wanted it too badly.

And besides, Ben had asked me to go out with him, after the gig.

✱✱✱ Seven

He had something to tell me, he said, something good. But we had to go and do something first. I didn't know what it was, what it would entail. To be honest, I didn't really care. Anything. I'd have done practically anything with Ben.

I had to own up to it; when he looked at me, especially as I was singing his songs, it – you know – did things to me, inside. I felt it every time. He felt it, too. I could feel him feeling it. We were feeling the same things, without ever having talked about it. That's how none of the others knew anything about us.

He waited until there was no one else around before he came up to me. 'What you doing afterwards, next Friday?' he said.

'Nothing,' I said, thinking, 'nothing but hurrying home before my mother loses her mind and trashes the whole house and my father rolls home from the wine bar and doesn't notice.' I didn't say any of that though; I just thought it. I thought other things too, at the same time. You know, like 'Mmm,' and 'Blimey,' and 'Help!' and 'Kiss Me Quick' and a thousand million other things, but said: 'Nothing,' while saying nothing.

'It's just,' he said, 'that I've got to go somewhere to see someone to sort something. I thought you might like to go with me?'

Might? Going somewhere with Ben to see someone to sort

something: now that sounded like my idea of a good time. Might didn't even enter into it. Definitely, was more like it. But: 'Where?' my mouth said, disconnected as it was from my brain.

'Well,' he said, 'that's, like, a bit difficult to say, at the moment. Why don't you wait and see, on Friday night? I can promise you, it'll be more than a bit interesting.'

And I was more than a bit interested. But Geoff wasn't going to go on stage, so he'd told Kirsty. We couldn't do without him, not this late in the day. He didn't, as it turned out, need to be so great on the keyboards; just as well: but he did need to know what to do and when. We none of us could do it without all the others. Even Kirsty was essential, at this late stage.

Poor Geoff was wandering about the school on his own when we eventually found him. He was trying to avoid everyone, including us; including Ben.

'Don't be such a wimp,' Kirsty said, before we could stop her. She walked off, shaking her head, about as compassionate as she ever got.

Geoffrey had gone into a permanent stutter. He was afraid, too nervous to put himself on the spot tonight. 'Y-you d-d-don't know wh-what it's b-been like,' he tried to say, looking to me for some sympathy, with Kirsten out of the way.

'Stick with me,' Beccs said, squaring up, much more like her old self, now her cousin wasn't there. 'Stick with me. I'm not scared of Stevens, or any of them.'

'N-no,' Geoff said. 'I'm n-not scared. It's just – they d-don't leave m-m-me alone. They don't.'

'I'll find Ben,' I whispered to Beccs. 'You keep your eye on him as much as you can.'

Beccs smiled. She nodded. 'I'll look after him,' she said. She sounded so secure, so ungirly. She was my friend. She was my best friend. I felt like hugging her. She wouldn't have appreciated it, although Kirsten hugged her all the time.

When I found Ben, he came bursting along the corridor as if he was about to start a fight. 'Where are they? I'll stuff their heads up their backsides! I'll break 'em, the bunch of w –'

'No,' I said, stopping him by holding my hands against his chest. He looked down at me. He wasn't that tall, but looked down at me in front of him with my hands pressed against his chest. 'No, that's no good,' I said. 'You'll be in trouble. Then we won't be playing tonight anyway. That's the important thing, Ben.'

My hands were still against him. He was still looking at me. This was the first time I'd touched him. We looked at each other as we always did, with so much unspoken understanding between us. The touch of my hands against his chest served only to heighten our mutual empathy.

'There's another way,' I said. 'But only you can make it happen.'

'Oh yes?' he said, amused. 'And what way's that?'

There are so many ways of skinning cats, but some are far more effective than others. When you're used to finding ways round people, as I was, you come to know all the best ploys. Ben had to talk to Kirsty, but alone. He had to get her to do everything I'd said, without telling her I'd said any of it. First he had to get her to agree to persuade Geoff to play that night.

'And how do I do that?' she'd said, he told me afterwards.

'Do you need me to tell you?' he'd asked. 'Kirsty, you could get any of us to do anything you wanted, surely you know that?'

69

She liked to think that, anyway. Hearing it from Ben was enough. She believed it. She thought Ben was no different from any of the others. The whole male population of the school fancied Kirsty; she wanted, more than anything, for Ben to be included in that.

'You could get any of us to do anything you wanted,' he told her, 'surely you know that?'

But the fact was, *he* could get any of the female population of the school to do whatever *he* wanted, whenever he wanted. He told her what he wanted her to do. She didn't want to do it, but she was only another part of the female population of the school; he could get her to do what he wanted, when he wanted.

She agreed. Naturally. She'd do as I said, exactly as I said, provided that I used Ben to pull her strings. Ben had more power than even he knew how to use. I knew how to use it though, believe me. I knew what we could achieve, Ben and me, together. We were going to make a success of this, if only for the one night of our school gig.

Kirsten agreed to do everything I'd said. She easily persuaded Geoff to play, promising him a surprise he'd like. She had to assure him, in every way she could, that he would like it. 'It's to do with you and me,' she told Geoff.

Geoff stammered: 'Y-y-y-you, a-a-a-'

'And me,' she said.

I wasn't there when she said it, but I knew what she said because that's what I told Ben to tell her to say, and how to say it; knowing full well what effect it would have on poor Geoffrey.

He had to agree, as he couldn't resist Kirsty. I played them one against the other, enjoying the game. I was good at it. I got Ben to tell Beccs she was the best in the band at football, which was just what the band needed. 'Be sporty,' he told her, because I told him to, to help give character to the band. 'Be sporty, Beccs,' he said, because I said, to give character to the band and to release some of Kirsty's hold over my best friend.

We went through it that day; believe me. Comments, people laughing at us. We let them laugh. We were coming together. This day had so much going for it. So much going for it, I wouldn't have been at all surprised if my dad had found himself another job. I didn't expect he would, not really; but we were good at facing the crowd, the threat of ridicule and the faint and fading possibility of trouble from the grunge-faction.

We shouldered it all, each in our own way. Ben remained oblivious. Geoff scarce. Kirsten's hair waved wildly. Beccs committed some very nasty fouls.

And me? I just wanted it. I wanted something from the evening, the night out with Ben, wherever we were going, whomsoever we were going to see.

We had everything prepared. Someone and his mate were going to work the lights for us. I got Kirsty and Beccs to organise that. I tell you, none of it would have happened, if not for me. I was, I am, responsible. I did it. I had something to prove, I think. I proved it. We proved it. From the moment we stepped out nervously onto that stage with the equipment ranged around, we were performers in a band: no more self-assured but infinitely more courageous than the crowd, shouting and slagging us all over the hall. From the moment Kirsten silenced the whole hall, as I had planned, by stepping over to Geoffrey and taking him in her arms and kissing him full on, on the mouth, we were above and beyond.

The grunge kicking truculent up the back of the hall were staggered, along with everybody else. The entire male population of the school fancied Kirsty. The entire female population knew it. And here she was, while the rest of Car Crime were shuffling and struggling through our nervousness, kissing Geoffrey Fryer full on the mouth. Geoff's reputation was guaranteed. His stature in the school and outside it would be elevated way above his old grunge associates. He was all right. You could tell from the look on his face that he was doing fine.

The whole hall faltered. The silence descended below the low level of our amplification equipment. Kirsty and Geoff unclenched. We all stood in our positions, prepared and ready. Everyone was waiting for us. There must have been more than two hundred faces looking up at us, darkening as the lights lowered, as our own were lit by the stage lights being operated from the back.

The lights went down. Our audience knew nothing, expecting what they were expecting. We let the moment last, holding it, drawing it out. I could feel my heart beating in my mouth. The low hum of the amplifiers reflected the feeling of tension we were all feeling, Car Crime and our audience. I looked about, held out my arms.

I screamed.

Eight

I screamed a scream the like of which you have never heard, believe me. Did I scream! We could all feel the shock of it, then the massive base beat that seemed to leap from the death of my scream and the furious over-beat and Geoff's maniac carsound keyboard racing through like a joy-rider gone crazy in a packed and shocked school hall.

The place erupted as Kirsty, Beccs and me leapt into our dance routines, which were too rough to actually be routines, but came and went as the car crime we were committing veered from one side of the stage to the other. The whole place and everyone in it went wild as the base beat crashed into them and our engines thrashed past dangerously. *This* they were not expecting. Neither were we, in a way. Our rehearsals in Geoff's granny-annexe had never sounded like this. There was never this level of sound, this sense of excitement. Ben kept the drumming going and going, with Geoffrey driving in and out of the spaces, driving the whole thing, including ourselves, Car Crime, and our accomplices dancing wildly all over the hall.

There was now no sign of any Grunge Mechanics as our stolen cars slowed, then slowed again, as the insistent drumming allowed everyone a space in which to cross safely. But NO!

I screamed again, just when everybody thought it was safe. I screamed as before; as before the driving drums drove us all

round the bend into a driven frenzy. We kept it going, as if
the police were following close behind. Their headlights were
reflected in our eyes. The lighting boys up the back had given
chase, caught up as they were in our crime-city race the
wrong way round the one-way streets. In the middle of the
road, quite unexpectedly, I screamed again. The tingles running down my spine were felt by everyone as the cars
careered wildly, almost out of control.

Then they slowed, coming down, coming down, until the
engines ticked, thrumming with slow threat. I stepped up to
the mike again. They were expecting a scream. Instead:

Whatever you do it's insane,
You can't look back.
Locked in the right hand lane,
You're on the wrong track.
What have you done?

Wherever you're going to
Keep your heel to the floor.
It's all over now, baby, for you,
They can't touch you any more.
What have you done?

Then Beccs, rapping:

Where can you go
  In the light of the truth
When the only thing you have
  Is your light and your youth
When your dreams are all on fire
  You have nothing
But your hot wires
  And your desire.
Keep your heel to the floor

It's all over now
They can't touch you any more.
What have you done?

Then back to me:

Whatever you do it's insane,
You can't look back.
Locked in the right hand lane,
You're on the wrong track.
What have you done?

Wherever you're going to
Keep your heel to the floor.
It's all over now, baby, for you,
They can't touch you any more.
What have you done?

We went round the circuit, once, twice, three times. We went round and round and round with the dizzying beat inside us, the roar of the engines driving us round, and round, and round again. We were, all of us, on a joy ride with hell to pay for our car crimes, experiencing the excitement of being out of control, or controlled by something faster and more powerful than ourselves or our own little lives. We were Car Crime. Thank you! We had never felt so good. We were Car Crime. And we were committed to it.

I had never felt so good. We were on a high, sailing furious from the stage somewhere a good way clear of the floor. No one had ever heard anything quite like it, including ourselves.

'That was something else,' Geoffrey exclaimed, without the

trace of a stutter. Kirsty was smiling at him. Beccs hugged me, as if we'd never been so close.

The hall was deserted by this time. The whole thing had only lasted about three quarters of an hour. That's all the time we were allowed. Which was a happy coincidence, as we didn't have enough material to keep going any longer. But three quarters of an hour found us overwhelmed with applause and whistles and cries for more. Not less, more! It was about a thousand times better than any of us had dared hope. These were our school-mates, don't forget. They were the ones we lived with every day, the ones as likely to put you down behind your back as they were to smile in your face. The whole of the two-faced school faced us at the end as a single unit of appreciation. They really liked us.

'They really liked us!' Beccs cried.

'They did!' Kirsty joined in. 'They really thought we were good.'

'W-we w-were good,' Geoff said.

I looked at Ben. So far he had said nothing. He was smiling, but as if all this was only to be expected. He was new to the school. He didn't know most of them like we did. They didn't know him.

'They liked your music, Ben,' I said.

'They liked *our* music,' he said.

Yes, we were at the start of something; this was going to be good. Everything was so fresh, new and exciting. This was special; we could all feel it.

We were all complimenting each other, telling each other how good we were, enjoying the adrenalin after-glow, when Ben's mobile went. He said a couple of okays into it, looked up at us and shrugged. 'Got to go,' he said. 'See you all next week, yeah?'

'Yeah,' the others said. Kirsty chanced giving him a pecky

little kiss on the cheek before he went. Beccs almost went for one, too, but lost her nerve at the last moment.

Me? I didn't do or say anything at all. Ben was supposed to be taking me somewhere to do something with someone or other. I'd been really looking forward to it. The excitement had elevated me, the disappointment dashing me too hard into the ground.

Ben was gone before I could really realise the full force of my disappointment. We started off from the hall, leaving the school with Kirsty and Beccs still riding high, with Geoffrey following on like Kirsty's lap-dog, hoping for another kiss before the evening was out. I was speechless, following up the rear, hopeless and confused. Ben and I were a fitting pair, the long and the short of it, a couple of misfits with everything in common but nothing at all to say to each other.

Then my mobile went. I struggled to fish it from my bag in time, fumbling and dropping it onto the pavement in front of me. The battery didn't fly out this time, luckily, as Ben's voice said, as soon as I'd retrieved the phone and pressed the button:

'Amy? It's me. You still with the others?'

'Yes,' I said.

'Right,' he said. 'Get away. Go to the big video shop in the parade. You know it?'

'Of course.'

'Good. I'll pick you up there.'

He went, that suddenly. The others were looking at me. 'It's my dad,' I said. 'I've got to go and meet him. Up the – in the town.'

'You want us to go with you?' Beccs said.

'No!' I said, too suddenly. 'No. It's all right. You go on. I'll see you – what, tomorrow? You going to town?'

'We might be,' Kirsty said. 'We haven't quite made up our minds yet.'

'All right,' I said to Beccs. 'Call me, yeah?'

'Yeah,' she said.

'See you,' I said, walking off in the other direction. My heart was pumping. I could feel them watching me as I went up the road. It was all I could do to prevent myself from running. I think they could all see I was lying, from the flush that must have appeared on my face. Not that I was attracted to Ben, or anything – yeah, *right*! I couldn't stop thinking about him, however much I hated fancying someone everyone else fancied. It made me the same as everyone else, just exactly the same.

The only difference was, and it was a big difference, Ben hadn't asked anyone else to go with him somewhere to meet someone and do something. No. He'd only asked me, little Amy Peppercorn, to do that; whatever it was.

It was only me he was smiling at from the open passenger window of a very nice car that was pulling up outside the video shop. It was just me he was saying hello to, telling me to get in the back seat of a black BMW with someone driving and talking on a mobile at the same time.

'This is Toby,' Ben was saying.

Toby was going: 'Yeah. Yeah. Yeah. OK. Got it,' into his mobile.

'Hello, Toby,' I said. 'Nice car.'

'Right,' Toby said, coming off the phone. 'Lorry Park, East Industrial Estate,' he said to Ben.

'Where we going?' I asked.

Toby looked over his shoulder at me. He was older than I was, but not by much. Not enough, surely, for a car like this. 'Lorry Park,' he said. 'East Industrial Estate.'

'What for?' I said.

Toby glanced at Ben. 'The Meet,' Ben turned and said.

Toby was back on the phone, going, 'Yep, got it. Lorry Park, East Industrial Estate. Yep. See ya.' He clicked from one call to the next, driving the car with one hand. I felt a bit uneasy about his lack of concentration, but the car was an automatic with a cream interior, and seemed to be used to being driven by someone with one hand and one ear pressed against a mobile.

Ben seemed different, sitting there nervy and snappy while Toby made one call after the next, all the same, one after the next. There was no mention of our school gig or any of the other Car Crime members. We were passengers, Ben and me, along for the ride, steered single-handedly towards some-where that was the East Industrial Estate by someone called Toby for something everyone on their mobiles seemed to want to know about.

Ben had his arm hooked round the back of the driver's seat. I tapped his elbow, wanting more attention, more acknow-ledgement than this. I wanted to know why we were off to that somewhere with this someone for whatever something was going to happen.

But Ben put his finger to his lips. His look asked me not to ask, so I kept it until I could see the lorry park and how populated it was with cars and bikes and people, but hardly any lorries to speak of. 'What's happening?' I had to ask as huge plumes of blue smoke struck up from between the wheels of souped cars and the smell of burning rubber came billowing into Toby's BMW.

'All right!' Toby exclaimed as we and several other cars swung into the lorry park. There were cars everywhere, back-wheel rubber burning where several people were holding up the back of a car, base-bound music pounding from the massive black box in-car stereos of wide white cabriolets. A Cadillac bounced slowly on its front wheels from one suspension-lowered super-stereo to the next. 'Hey, man!' Toby was yelling out of his open window, high-fiving as we went through the car crowd.

'What do you think?' Ben said, turning to me. His face was flushed, his eyes glistening with excitement.

'What's happening?' I said, looking round at everything and everyone.

'It's a town-race,' Ben said.

'Hey, Gonzo!' Toby was shouting out of the window.

'They go for it, a ton, ton-twenty round the ring road. Imagine, all these cars.'

Yes, I was thinking, all these cars. So many. The huge lorry park was full. I couldn't believe what I was seeing.

'Wheels, man!' Toby was shouting.

'This is mad,' I was saying. 'Who arranges all this?'

'Everyone,' Ben said.

'And no one,' Toby chipped in over his shoulder, before going back to shouting at everyone out of his window. 'Fat-Nuts! Ya heap! Get back down the breakers!'

'This is mad,' I said.

'It's the next thing,' Ben said, with the nervous excitement still glistening in his eyes.

'You have to experience this. Sheer Car Crime.'

'What?' I said, nervously. I didn't much like the intensity of the look in Ben's eyes. Suddenly I didn't care so much for Car Crime. 'What are we going to do?'

Toby's mobile went again. He flipped it open while Ben watched my expression. 'Yep!' Toby yapped, while Ben looked for a reaction in me. 'Oh, sh – now? Right!' Toby slammed, flinging his mobile into his lap. He swung the car round, very nearly hitting two or three people. 'Pig Patrol!' he yelled out of the window. 'Next venue! Hey, Fat-Nuts, follow man! The Law!'

We were picking up speed as we approached the lorry park exit, grinding to a halt as other cars turned and followed us far too closely. Toby screeched away from the park as sirens and headlights began to appear from the other direction. The light was fading into the evening as we sped away, sweeping round the bend, followed by at least half a dozen other boy and girl racers.

'What's happening?' I was saying, being tossed from one side of the back seat to the other.

'The filth!' Toby yelled.

'The police,' yelled Ben. 'It's all right. We're well away.'

'No we ain't,' Toby said, as a convoy of police headlights blazed by on the other side of the road.

Ben's head swung round to watch them drive past.

'They'll be turning,' Toby said. 'Leave it to me,' he said, with his foot driving harder into the floor of the BMW.

'What's wrong?' I said to Ben. He didn't answer me. I began to feel afraid. I could feel the speed increasing, pressing me into the back of my seat.

'What do you think?' Ben said to Toby, as he swung the car off the main road. There was a line of about six or seven of us making our way too quickly, far too quickly, up a very small lane between the fields and trees. The car was bouncing, so was I. My head touched the roof once or twice.

'Short cut!' Toby yelled, pulling into the gated entrance to a field.

'Where we going?' I shouted. I was holding onto the back of Ben's seat, trying to pull myself forward to look out of the windscreen. I could see some tents up ahead in the dusk, with a few people stopping in the field to see what was happening. 'This is a camp site!'

Toby whooped like a rodeo cowboy as the BMW slewed over the grass between the tents. Ben was also shouting, the two of them like a pair of very excited brats playing a danger-ous car-chase video game.

I glanced behind at the line of cars skidding through the tents. One guy-rope was dragged away by a bumper, the tent falling and trailing after it. The enraged campers were run-ning out, gesticulating, picking up children, throwing sticks and tent pegs at the cars.

'This is sick!' I screamed.

The wailing boys couldn't hear me, so ecstatic were they, so carried away by the wheel skids and the mud and the speed of getting away with everything.

We came out the other side between the trees onto a little lane quite dark in the dusk in the woods. Our headlights were blazing, lighting up the tunnel through the trees. All the way behind us headlights blazed, hooters blared. We were in a wildly excited convoy, travelling too fast round the sweep of a little country lane with the light fading in the leaves.

'Slow down!' I shrieked. 'Slow down! Anything could be coming round one of these bends. What's the matter with you?'

'What's the matter with her?' Toby said.

'It's all right,' Ben said, turning in his seat, 'Toby knows what he's doing.'

'Does he? I bet those people in the camp site don't think so. This is a nightmare, Ben. Why did you bring me here, to all this? Ben, this is just sick! What are we supposed to be run-ning away from, anyway? What's happening?'

'Does a lot of joy-riding, your bitch, does she?' Toby said to Ben.

'What?' I said. 'What?'

'It's all right,' Ben said. 'Tobe knows what he's doing.'

'Listen, Tobe,' I said, leaning forward as far as I could go.

'Listen. I do not do joy-riding – and I am not his *bitch*! Do you understand?'

Toby shrugged. He had, at least, greatly decreased his speed. 'Chill,' he said.

'It's all right,' Ben started to say.

'No!' I said. 'No, it's not. If by joy-riding, your mate, *Tobe*, means to say that this car is stolen, then it's not all right. It's anything but all right.'

'You gonna shut her up,' Toby said.

'No one's gonna shut me up!' I screamed. 'Now stop this car and let me out! Stop, right now!'

Toby pulled over. We were in the middle of nowhere, pulling short of the main A-road between the towns at dusk on a busy Friday night.

'I should have known this wasn't your car!' I was yelling as I got out, slamming the door. The drivers in the other cars behind us were hanging their heads out to hear what I was saying. 'You're all car thieves!' I shouted at them.

Ben was getting out beside me. 'Come back,' he said, 'please, Amy.'

'No,' I said. 'I'm not getting back in there.'

Toby was already beginning to pull away. The other cars were following. We watched them to the end of the road, where they turned left into the main flow of the traffic. We were left standing silently on the grass verge of a little lane in the middle of nowhere.

I looked at Ben, shaking my head in disbelief. 'How could you do that to me? They're all car thieves,' I said again.

'They're Car Criminals,' Ben said.

I was staring at him.

'That's what I thought we were,' he said.

✳✳✳ Nine

'**W**here've you been?' my dad whined, as soon as I came in. He had a baby fast asleep slumped across his chest on the settee; the other was asleep on the floor.

'Joy-riding,' I said.

'What time is it?' he said, looking up at me, as if I went joy-riding every other Friday evening until this late.

'It's not late,' I said. 'Considering.' Considering the wild car rides, I felt like saying, the screaming I'd done in the back of the car, the screaming I'd done at Ben as he'd tried to get us a cab, the stolid silence all the way home in the back.

'Don't go in yet,' Ben had tried to say to me as the cab pulled up outside our house, 'it's early yet.'

'It's late enough for me!' I'd slammed, shutting him down again.

'Well it feels late to me,' my dad said. 'It always feels late, to me. I can't do this. I can't do what your mother wants me to –'

'They're not even ready for bed,' I said, looking at the girls as they lay like flung rag-dolls, their little bare limbs out at all angles.

'I can't do it,' he said. 'Amy, they run rings round me. I can't – they just won't let me, you know?'

'They're the same for everyone, Dad,' I said, putting down my things, so I could pick up some of the other things that were scattered all over the floor. 'What *is* all this stuff?' I said, picking up a broken ashtray I'd never seen before in my life. Across the room, I noticed something that looked like a hank of hair from a cat. Down one of the walls hung, quite decoratively, something that I could only describe as the attachments from a pig's eye. 'What's that?' I squirmed. 'This is disgusting.'

'I know,' he said. 'Don't ask me anything. I can't remember what's happened in here tonight. I can't put them down. They won't let me dress them. I'm useless, Amy, useless. And now your mother wants me to –'

'Come on,' I said, picking the twin from my dad's feet, 'let's try and get them to bed, shall we?'

He sighed. 'I'm useless at this. It was all different with you. You weren't like this at all. There was only one of you.'

Joanna started to cry as the telephone rang. She screamed into the mouthpiece as I picked up the receiver. 'Dad!' I bellowed. 'Dad! Take Jo, will you?'

'I can't!' he cried, wrestling with Georgina, who had woken with a screaming start as the phone went and her sister fired up. Our whole house went from tranquillity to bedlam in one ring of the telephone, into which I was having to shout: 'Hello!'

'Amy,' a voice came back.

'Just a minute,' I cried. I dumped the other twin on Dad, who was trying to stem the flow of blood from one of his nostrils. 'Here,' I said, overloading him with twins.

'I think she's scratched my nose,' he said, bleeding. 'Amy, my nose is bleeding.'

'Amy,' Ben's voice said, as I placed the telephone receiver to my ear, 'I've got to see you. I shouldn't have let you go in like that.'

'You shouldn't have done a lot of things, Ben. I told you, I don't want to talk about it. I just can't – how you could even –

85

Look,' I said, 'my dad's nose is bleeding, all right? Can you hear what it's like here? Go away, Ben.'

'No, Amy, I'm not going to. I'm coming over, all right?'

'No, it's not all right.'

'I'm coming over anyway.'

'Oh do what you like. I just don't care,' I said. 'Come over if you want to be bled over, if you want to change some nappies. Come over, why don't you?'

I put the phone down on him. I didn't have time to stand there arguing about it. Dad was bleeding profusely over everything he possibly could. He seemed to be bleeding as much as he could, deliberately. Nobody could have bled that much without making an effort.

I didn't have time to think about Ben and what had happened; I was too busy cleaning all the babies in the house and feeding them and plugging their noses and putting bibs and bloodied shirts in the soak-bucket my mum kept for all the nastier stains that only bleach or fire could get out. There wasn't time to think about Ben, and how he could possibly have thought it was right to take me there, for that. I was just too busy to let Ben get to me, but he got to me. I couldn't stop thinking about it, however busy I was.

My mum came in tasting of wine and conversation, all relaxed and nearly happy after her evening out. But my dad was a bundle of nerves as he tried to force another nosebleed to show just how badly he had suffered with the babies without their mother. He kept glancing at me, nervously jealous of his wife's good humour. I ran out as soon as the doorbell rang.

Ben came ringing on the bell and knocking on the front door, asking to be let in, as my relaxed mother laughed at her husband's bleeding nose as a poor excuse for not letting her go back to work. 'Did you find a job today?' I could hear her asking.

'Can't I come in?' Ben was saying to me, standing on the doorstep.

I glanced over my shoulder. 'What for?' I said.

'Because I have,' I heard her saying.

'I need to talk to you,' Ben said.

'Well, I don't need to talk to you,' I said.

'What do you mean?' my dad was saying.

'Amy,' Ben said, looking at me. Looking at me, he said, 'We do need to talk.'

'You found me a job?' my dad said.

'Come in here,' I sighed, keeping Ben to the hall.

'What sort of a job,' my dad was saying, 'have you found me?'

'Listen,' Ben said, 'it was my fault.'

'No,' my mum was saying, 'I found *me* a job.'

'I know,' I said, 'you told me all that in the cab. I know it was your fault.'

'What do you mean?' – my father.

'No, listen,' Ben said, 'I made a mistake. I thought you were – I thought – I don't know what I thought.'

'A job!' – my mother. 'A job. Don't you know what one of those is? No wonder you lose them so easily.'

I was listening to everyone at once, not able to concentrate properly on anything. One of the twins murmured upstairs. That was all I needed.

'I know what one of them is!' – my dad. 'I've been looking. I've been looking.'

'I wanted,' Ben said, 'to do something else – to experience something. Car Crime. It fitted in, all that. That's all.'

'While I've been finding! There's a nice little teaching post going that I could walk into as easily as – as easily as you can walk out of your jobs.' – my mum.

'Well it didn't fit in with me,' I said.

'That's not fair!' – my father.

'No,' said Ben, 'I know. It was a mistake. I'm sorry.'

'Fair?' – my mother, her relaxation and conversation evaporating rapidly. 'Fair? What's fair got to do with anything?'

'I'm sorry,' Ben said. 'It wasn't right for me, either. I just thought it was – kind of, necessary.'

'I'll get a job!' – my father.

'When?' – my mother.

'The thing is,' Ben said, 'I don't want to lose you.'

'When?' – my father. 'When do you think? As soon as I can find one!'

'As a friend,' Ben said.

'And what if you can't find one?' – my mum.

'Friends?' Ben said, reaching out and touching my hand.

'What?' I said.

'Then it's not my fault,' – my mum.

'Friends?' Ben said, taking my hand.

'Then it'll be my fault, I suppose?' – my mum.

'Friends,' I said, as Ben pulled me to him.

'No!' – my dad. 'Nothing's your fault, is it! It's all mine. Always has been.'

'Yes!' – my mum.

'Yes,' Ben said, holding me to him.

· I could feel Ben's face against my own. I could feel his breath in one ear. In the other, my mum and dad starting to shout at each other. In another, in my third and fourth ears, my sisters firing up upstairs. Ben – Ben Lyons was holding me, his face touching mine, while the bedlam of my home crowded into all my real and imaginary ears, crowding out my senses.

'We need to concentrate on the band,' Ben said, pulling far enough away to look closely into my face. 'I know a man,' he said.

'Yes!' – my mum. 'All right! Yes, it's always been your fault. You could have –'

'Oh!' – my dad. 'That's it. Blame me! Blame me!'

'I know a man who can get us some studio time,' Ben said. 'That's what I was wanting to tell you about.'

The twins were cranking up upstairs, rattling the bars of their cots and the windows of every room in the house.

'Who else can I blame?' – my mum. 'If there's no money coming in, who else can I blame – Amy?'

'Amy?' Ben said, trying to make himself heard.

'Whah!' – Joanna.

'Whah! Whah!' – Georgina.

'Amy?' – my dad. 'Don't bring Amy into it. It's nothing to do with Amy.'

'Whah!'

'Whah! Whah!'

'Amy? Fifteen hundred quid gets us four hours' studio time. Let's make a recording, shall we?'

'Whah!'

'Whah! Whah!'

'Anyway,' – my dad, 'Amy agrees with me!'

'About what?'

'About everything. What else?'

'You always think Amy agrees with you!'

'So do you!'

'Whah! Whah! Whah!'

'Well she doesn't!'

'No, she doesn't!'

'That's only three hundred quid each, from the five of us. Let's do it. Can you get three hundred quid, Amy?'

'She agrees with me!'

'No she doesn't!'

'Yes she does!'

'No she does not!'

'Ask her then!'

'I will!'

'So will I!'

'Whah! Whah! Whah!'

'Can you get three hundred, Amy?' Then he kissed me, gently, on my closed mouth. His lips were so very soft, so very warm they hardly touched me.

'I could ask my parents,' I started to say.

'Whah! Whah! Whah!' wailed the kids: all of them.

✳✳✳Ten

Ben kissed me and I missed it. My mad family spoiled what should have been one of the best experiences of my life so far. It was as if I wasn't even there, as if my place had been taken by the screaming and the shouting taking place all around us.

The band rehearsed twice a week, improving all the time, adding stuff to our 'repertoire', as Kirsten and my dad wanted to call it.

My dad was hanging round the house nearly all the time now. He couldn't get a job. He was walking about, supposedly doing odd jobs, bits of decorating and stuff; but mostly he was feeling sorry for himself. He kept looking over at me with that sorry-for-himself look, hoping I'd join in. He kept trying to corner me, to talk me into being on his side. 'No one could expect me to look after Jo and George all day, on my own, every day, could they? Amy, you wouldn't like it, would you?'

'Does he think I like being on my own here looking after babies all day?' my mum would corner me and ask.

'I will find a job, Amy,' my dad kept trying to tell me. 'There are plenty of jobs out there for fit and intelligent men like me.'

I'd never thought of my dad as being particularly fit, or intelligent; but, maybe I'm not the best person to ask.

'He's going to find it more and more difficult,' my mum

tried to confide in me, 'at his age. He still thinks he's a young man.'

Meanwhile, I'd been getting so far behind with my studies, I wouldn't dare ask my mother for help. She'd find me out. Instead of asking for my approval, she'd throw a wobbler and a half, looking round for things to blame: my dad, the band. My dad would be in even bigger trouble than he was, and life would be intolerable without the band. So I kept quiet, letting them both come to me in turns, asking me to be on their side, while I quietly failed at becoming a doctor, or anything that would require any qualification beyond my ordinary GCSEs.

'And then there's the money,' my mum kept wanting to tell me.

'We've still got money,' my dad tried to insist, as if spending their savings like this didn't matter. 'It doesn't matter,' he tried to reassure me, and himself, 'I'll soon get a good job. We'll have some savings back again in no time.'

'We can't keep living on our savings for long,' my mum worried at me. 'It's ridiculous, isn't it, Amy, when I could go for that job, just like that? Isn't it ridiculous?'

It would have been ridiculous to ask them for three hundred pounds at the moment, just for a few hours' hiring of a sound studio. I'd asked Ben if we couldn't just get the studio for the hour. 'That'd be enough time,' I went and said, like an idiot, 'to lay down a couple of tracks, wouldn't it?'

We were having a break from our rehearsal in Geoff's granny-annexe. His mum kept popping up with bottles of 'pop'. 'Did I hear someone screaming earlier?' she always

92

asked, with that long and worried face on her. 'Is everyone all right, I wonder?'

'We're all fine, Mrs Fryer,' I'd have to assure her, with poor Geoffrey fried red and curly as a crisp.

'Thanks for the pop,' Beccs would call after her. 'Mmm,' she'd say, 'don't I just love a good drop of pop,' as she flipped the top from a can of coke.

They were riding high on the idea of making proper demo tapes in a real recording studio. Ben had told them about it, looking at me, just as he had before. He'd kissed me: I'd missed it. I was no joy-rider; neither was he, he said. He looked at me as he told the others three hundred quid each, and the afternoon's ours. But I had to go and suggest like an idiot that an hour would do to lay down a couple of demo tracks. Ben looked at me then, in another way. What an idiot I was.

'There'll be all kinds of sound technicians and a studio manager with mixing equipment to set up for us, or it won't work properly.'

Kirsten was looking at me too. They all were, but Kirsten had copied and exaggerated Ben's expression to make me look a right and proper fool. 'We might as well go and tape ourselves in Becky's garage,' she said, as if she knew anything at all about sound technicians and mixing equipment.

I'd said what I'd said because of the three hundred, because of my dad and my mum sneaking up to me in turns to complain each about the other and about hard luck and about money. Money, money, money. Somebody had to make some. In our house, at the moment, all we did was spend. Spend, spend, spend. I couldn't possibly go to them for any concentrated help with my homework, let alone to ask for three hundred pounds they really didn't have to pay for something neither I nor certainly Kirsten properly understood.

'Couldn't we just pay for the hour?' I asked, then bitterly regretted it. I had to tell the others I had no chance of raising three hundred quid this side of my twenty-first birthday, or possibly even longer. I was probably going to end up jobless, like my dad, or stacking shelves in the supermarket for just under three hundred pounds a year after overtime.

'Well,' Ben said, almost straight away, 'I can raise four, if it comes to it.' He said that looking at me like a mate from school who'd never kissed me in his life.

'So can I,' said Kirsty, pretty well straight away afterwards, looking at Ben most unlike a school friend, her face ready to kiss and be kissed at any moment.

'And me,' Geoff said, looking at Kirsty like someone recently kissed, who'd like to be kissed again, and again, and again.

'That's it then,' Beccs said, giving a little burp, like the antidote to all that kiss-wishing, at the end of her cola-can. 'That's enough money between us. Let's do it.'

So four, four and a bit weeks later, we did it. It was just as Ben had said: there were sound technicians and a studio manager with cans over their ears. We all had to do our bit, so they could adjust to our equipment and our voices and mix it all up afterwards. It was surprisingly hard work. Not at all like rehearsing round at Geoff's or performing on the stage at school. We had to wait around for ages while nobody seemed to be doing anything at all; then we had to be ready instantly, only to find out we weren't.

Geoff had the kind of sweat on a short person like me could drown in. Beccs turned up in her football kit, then changed into her little skirt, then changed back into her football kit.

She was trying to please everyone at once. We were all too nervous to reassure each other. Kirsten was a real bitch, of course. She kept wondering if Geoff's fingers weren't going to be too wet to play properly, if Becky could possibly do her rapping bits and keep her bum still at the same time, and if my voice wasn't going to sound just a little bit vacant without a great echoing hall round it. She left Ben alone.

Ben got himself tangled with the sound technicians as soon as he arrived, drinking coffee with the studio manager as if he knew everyone and did this sort of thing all the time.

It was Ben that clapped us all together to start before we were ready. We'd spent our time worrying and dripping, arguing and bitching and getting changed again and again. Ben clapped his hands when the studio manager raised his long, long thumbs. Everybody there was tall and very thin, long-thumbed and balding, with ponytails and black tee shirts, and black jeans with studded belts. We looked like a bunch of fresh-faced kids, because that's what we were. These old, tired music business faces had seen it all before. They seemed to want to go out of their way to let us know it.

'What do you want me to do, Ben?' Kirsty was saying, her hair swaying like a younger, blonder, cleaner version of the sides and back of the studio manager's head. Ben wanted Kirsty to look beautiful most of the time, coming in every now and then with her little, long-haired backing vocals.

'I want you to look after Geoff for me,' I heard Ben saying to Kirsty. 'I don't think he can hack it without someone cool like you to look after him. Can you do that for me?'

I saw Ben looking at Kirsten. After a look like that, she'd do anything he said. I could hear her excited intake of breath from where I was, way over the other side of the studio, minding my own business. But not minding my own business. I was watching Ben to see how he was looking at

95

Kirsten. I wanted to be sure. I was sure: he didn't look at her how he'd looked at me. That look was my own, entirely.

Beccs was watching me. I looked away from Ben and Kirsten to find her studying me not minding my own business. She smiled as I noticed her there. I smiled back at her. A moment of silent communication passed between us.

I turned away, annoyed. It angered me that she'd seen something of the way I think I felt about Ben. Beccs seeing it turned it into nothing more than a similarity to every other girl in our school: certainly similar to every other girl in our band, including Kirsten. That's how Ben, boys like Ben, got us, made us all the same with their looks and their smiles and their way of drawing each of us in. I seemed to have held out the longest; he'd had to actually ask me out in a stolen car with a real car criminal to try to win me over. He'd actually given me a little kiss on the lips, which I'd actually missed and he'd evidently forgotten about. Since then, nothing. No more smiles, no special looks, certainly no touches, or kisses. Or kisses. Nothing.

Beccs caught me looking at him as he was giving a smile to Kirsten. She knew now, which was not good. I could no longer trust her not to be a first cousin to Kirsten above being best friends with me. Once we could have shared our feelings, our emotions, keeping them between ourselves. Now I had to turn away from her for fear of having the way I felt held up and examined for flaws, for height and length of hair and shape of leg and fairness of face; the very things Beccs most feared herself. It wasn't fair: she'd have still been safe with me. I still wouldn't have subjected her to all that, for fear of hurting her.

Ben clapped us all to attention. We had the cans positioned over our ears. In mine, the familiar electric buzz of the equipment awaiting my voice. None of us were ready in our discomfort and our nervousness, but the sound of silent sound-equipment hummed in our ears. Kirsten touched Geoffrey on the hand because she was told to, to calm him. The sound engineer on the other side of the glass panels held up his thumbs.

We missed it. Everyone looked at each other. Ben made a sign, looked at me. The sound engineer looked up again, stuck up his thumbs.

I screamed.

'Blimey!' the studio manager exclaimed.

✳✳✳Eleven

You'd have thought we'd signed for one of the big record labels, the way Kirsten went round all week telling everybody about the recording studio. She didn't bother telling them that we'd paid – that they'd paid – fifteen hundred quid for it. We were suddenly pop stars in and out of the studio recording our stuff for our first album.

In fact, our stuff sounded very different on tape, at the end of that day. It kind of lost something in its translation through the recording equipment.

'It doesn't sound right,' I said to Ben.

He smiled. 'Listen,' he said, turning up the volume. It still didn't sound right, but was a whole lot better.

'I think you can hear what we look like,' Kirsten said.

I looked at Beccs, who ignored the remark. It was a typical, dumb-blonde Kirsten thing to say; more than that, it simply wasn't true. I sounded a whole lot bigger than I was, for sure. Geoff sounded as if he sometimes knew what he was doing. Kirsty sounded in tune and with impeccable timing. Beccs sounded a lot like her old lost self, tough and determined. Only Ben sounded anywhere near right, as every sound was his in essence, if not belonging to, then owing everything to him. He was the creative one.

Kirsten went round as if she'd put a band together herself and now stood poised on the threshold of stardom. Geoff went round as if he was in Kirsty's band; in other words, going out with her. Beccs went round trying to become a Becky. Ben went round on his own, not a loner, but creatively way beyond everybody else. And I went round the bend.

My dad couldn't find another job, not one with enough money, anyway. He couldn't support us: unlike my mother. She could, and did, get a good teaching position; but had to travel to a school in another district entirely, where they were looking for a head of department. She was up early in the morning, home late in the evening. But she was suddenly very full of new energy. She collected her old self where she'd left it hanging up with her teaching clothes in the wardrobe, and put it back on. She stepped out of the house on her first morning back at work, wearing her old self on her sleeve with a smile on her face; a smile that she was struggling to prevent from turning into a smug grin as the twins cried to see their mother dressed and going out through the front door.

My dad nearly cried too, at the same sight. He sagged at the kitchen table with the washing-up and the laundry ranged round him in mixed piles. Plates and socks and frozen nappies were in the sink.

'Frozen nappies?' I said.

He nodded, as if no further explanation was necessary. Such things were already a fact in the madness of this house. The beginning of his first day on his own and he was already rehearsing his total breakdown with rock hard disposable pads and a bin full of liquid ice cream. 'What do you call melted ice cream?' he turned to me and said.

I shrugged.

'Cream,' he said, then turned away. He was still wearing his old dressing gown as he gazed for a long time into the bin. 'I can't do this,' he said. 'I know I can't. How can I keep this place clean and do all that – everything?' He stood up, picking one of the twins from her high chair. He looked at the wetness in the palm of his hand. 'Do me a favour?' he said. 'Put a nappy in the microwave for me, will you?'

So I was late for school. Very late. I had a note from my father, which he'd written in a very unsteady hand when I'd got back from the shops with the new nappies. All the way to school I'd been thinking about how much I didn't want to go. I wanted to want to go, but couldn't any longer find anything I enjoyed about school. I wanted to see Beccs, and Ben, of course, but at the same time I didn't want everyone looking at me as if I was a part of Kirsten's little crew, one of her few mates, a member of her pop band.

My work had got so bad; I was so far behind. I knew I couldn't carry on like I had been. My mother was a teacher again, so maybe she'd still be able to help me. Now she had some of her old self-esteem back, she could perhaps give me the pictures I needed to catch up, or at least not fail all three A-levels so dismally.

But as soon as I got to school, I forgot all about my lack of maths understanding as I tried to figure out what all the excitement was about. Everyone was looking at me, as if there was something I should know that I didn't know. There was plenty I didn't know; the differentiation of trigonometrical functions, for one thing. But I didn't think it could have been that; this lot didn't know that, either. There were only a few of us in the whole school doing A-level maths, and I couldn't see any of the others. Too busy swotting, probably. Too busy getting ahead of me. Not difficult.

But there certainly was something. As I entered my biology lesson late, very late, with my rusk-stained excuse-me note, the whole class turned and looked at me. 'Do you know what melted ice cream's called?' I said. They gazed at me. 'Cream,' I said.

'Yes,' said Mrs McKintyre, my Biology tutor, 'very logical. Have you finished your assignment?'

I hadn't finished my assignment. I hadn't been working on anything properly for weeks. I was useless. This couldn't go on. Everyone was looking at me; they could all see how useless I was.

It was only a little while before the lesson ended. I made no progress, in such a short space of time. The short space seemed like a long time though, ticking along with no progress made minute after minute till the hour's end and the bell going for break time.

Beccs and Kirsty were waiting right outside for me. 'Where've you been?' Beccs said.

'I had to go to the –' I started to say, but Kirsten was posing and pouting as if this was a catwalk between all my gaping Biology classmates. 'What's wrong with her?' I asked Beccs.

'Haven't you seen Ben?' Kirsten said, flicking, flicking, posing, pouting.

'No. Why?'

Beccs stepped forward and gave me a hug. Then Kirsten did the same thing. I had to stand there and wait while they took turns. I didn't know what I should be doing in return.

'They want to see us,' Kirsten announced.

'They want to see the band!' Beccs said.

They stood in front of me, the first cousins, grinning as people passed and looked at us in the corridor.

'Who wants to see us?' I said.

'A record company,' they said.

***✦Twelve

Ben kissed me. I kissed him. Kirsten kissed Ben. Beccs kissed him. But Ben kissed me. Geoff tried to kiss Kirsty.

We were ecstatic. I couldn't believe it could have happened so quickly. 'How can it happen so quickly?' I said.

'Contacts,' Ben said. 'I know a man who knows a man who knows an A and R man.'

'As simple as that?' I laughed.

'What's an A and R man?' Kirsty asked.

I'd like to be able to say that was another of Kirsten's dumb-blonde questions. I'd like to be able to say that; of course, I can't. She was only asking the question we'd all have asked if only we were honest, or dumb, enough. None of us, except Ben, knew what an A and R man was.

'Artists and Repertoire,' Ben said. 'And they can recognise talent when they hear it, Artists and Repertoire men.'

Kirsty nodded. I tried to look as if I already knew. Artists and Repertoire. That's what we were: artists with a repertoire. We were going to perform our stuff for the A and R man at Solar Records.

'Solar Records!' Ben exclaimed.

'Solar Records!' we recited, marching about, slapping each other as if we'd made it, big time.

You'd think we'd made the big time, the way Kirsten went round offering autographs, promising signed photographs to the laughing boys, giving out clothes and make-up advice to all the younger girls. She was lapping it up, all the attention and the admiration. Mind you, we all were. Even me.

There's something about the way people look at you, when they think there's something special about you. It all actually makes something special of you. First of all there's this feeling of disbelief, which goes away and leaves only the excitement. That's exactly what you get to see on people's faces. They don't believe it at first, then they do. You can see they do, as you can see their jealousy, which translates into your excitement and makes you more special still.

We all started behaving differently. We were more together during the day, when people would see us. Sometimes we were five, we were Car Crime walking about, a unit of significance, our own unit of achievement. Mostly though, we were four, the three of us girls, with Geoffrey, looking long in our background. We laughed a lot. In fact, we couldn't stop. Well, Geoff could, but Geoff never really laughed much at anything.

Beccs had stopped playing football altogether. It didn't matter. Maths didn't matter. Kirsty's long hair didn't get on my nerves any longer. In fact, I quite liked it. I started to like Beccs, Becky, in her shorter skirts. It looked kind of all right, kind of right now, for what we were. We were different, much more together, enjoying the attention we felt we deserved.

It was such a high. All day and all night it was on my mind. Next week, only next week, just about three weeks after our studio recording, we were going to the Solar Recording Studios to do our stuff for their main A and R man. Artists and Repertoire. I couldn't stop thinking about it. Whenever I did stop thinking about it, for a second or so, the feeling of it would still be with me. Then I'd remember again, to a feeling, a rush of excitement that could nearly take my breath away.

I kissed Ben whenever I saw him now. So did Kirsty and Beccs – Becky. Geoff hung looming long and indistinct in our

103

background. Ben was always working on new material. He had a million and one ideas, all at once. 'What we could do, is this,' he would say, before bombarding us with more and more Car Crime ideas of the joys of joy-riding, the excitement and the danger of stolen cars and speed. The others listened enthralled. I had to step back as Ben bubbled with enthusiasm and ideas, most of which I wondered if he hadn't come across from experience, despite his assurances to me that car crime, real car crime, wasn't right for him. He'd been taking quite a few days away from school. So had Geoffrey, but not as many as Ben.

The excitement of what was happening, what was actually happening, allowed me to put the reality of the car criminals to the back of my mind. Whatever everybody had to do, whatever they were like, was all worth it. The fact that we could make new music that the top Artists and Repertoire manager at Solar Records would want to hear, that we were a band that the A and R man wanted to see – nothing could compare to it. Anything else – everything else could be sorted out at some other time. We had a performance to perfect, a stage act that was like no other, each Car Crime performance a brand new offence to add to the unsolved city crime statistics.

That was Ben talking, by the way. He had a way of talking that put everything into the road-raged perspective of the car criminal. He had to be looking for inspiration somewhere, had to be. It made me feel uneasy, but where would we be without it? Peter Stevens and Michael Bradshaw and The Grunge Machine showed us where we'd be without it. They were a laughing stock, without even the power to persecute or to intimidate the likes of our poor stuttering Geoffrey. We laughed at them all the time, Becky, Kirsty and me. Geoffrey didn't. Geoffrey just didn't, did he? He was still too nervous to really enjoy being the centre of attention for a while. It didn't seem to be in him. Ben was, what can you say, slightly impervious to everything. Becky, Kirsty and me though, we were our school's Children of Destiny; that's what we were. Everywhere we went, we were what our greater destiny was going to make of us. Everyone watched us, envied us, wishing they were a part of what we were. They weren't it though; we were. *We* were it. We *were* it. We were *it*!

We were nearly famous; so famous, in fact, that Mrs McKintyre, my Biology tutor, started to take too much notice of me. I was too well known to blend in as I had in the past. She had to come over to me, asking if I was all right.

All right? *Was I all right?* I couldn't even answer her.

'It's just,' she said, 'I've been hearing about what's been happening to you. And the group.'

'Group?' I said.

'Your singing group,' she said.

'Oh,' I said, 'our singing group.'

'Yes. I've heard all about your concert in the hall a few weeks ago.'

'Concert? Hardly a concert.'

'Well, whatever you call it, it went down rather well, I hear.'

'Yes,' I said. 'Rather well.'

'Yes. You must have to practise, to rehearse quite a bit, I suppose, do you?'

'Quite a bit.'

'Mmm,' she said, looking right into me. I didn't like it, being looked into like that. It was too probing, too personal, a look like that, coming from a teacher. Teachers, I'd always liked to keep at arm's length; they were more likely to flatten my learning pictures than to colour them. Teachers were for classes, not for individuals. They were not my mother; they never understood how learning happened with me, or why it could fall flat and fail.

Mrs McKintyre sat looking into me a long, long time, before she said: 'How do you feel your work is going? Your school work?' – adding that last sentence as if I probably wouldn't have understood that my Biology tutor was talking about my studies.

'Okay, I think,' I said, unconvincingly.

Mrs McKintyre sat unconvinced by my side. 'Are you sure,' she said, 'that your concentration hasn't been – what can I say – diverted?'

Interviews like this made me nervous. I could feel the blood draining from my face. I couldn't look at her. She was making it impossible to look at her by staring into me in that way. She was asking too much of me. I felt like telling her to mind her own business.

'Amy?' she said, so softly, that I could feel the importance of her concern. She was measuring her voice and her words to give me all kinds of other, unspoken messages. She wanted to make me feel guilty. Her quiet voice wanted to tell me that failing was my fault, my own and nobody else's.

'Amy?'

I looked at her again, for at least a moment.

'Ben Lyons is a bit of a dish,' she said, 'isn't he?'

A bit of a dish? *A bit of a dish*? Which century is it that teachers all seem to choose to live in? 'Is he?' I said.

'Don't you find him attractive?' Mrs McKintyre asked.

This was just too embarrassing for words. I shrugged; it was all I *could* do.

'I'm sure you do,' she went on. 'As do about half the girls in the whole school.'

I shrugged again.

'The thing is,' she said, 'the thing is, your work isn't up to its old standard, Amy, is it? I want you to face up to the fact that something seems to be going wrong with your studies. Am I right?'

I looked down, nodding slightly.

'I'm worried about you, Amy,' she said. Then she didn't say anything, for ages and ages. Time, when it goes by like that, gets louder and louder, shouting in your ears to say something.

'Aren't you going to say something?' Mrs McKintyre finally said, as it was becoming more and more obvious that I wasn't going to.

'Yes,' I said. 'I'm just – I think it's –'

'Look at me,' she said.

I did. She didn't make it easy, but I looked at her.

'Something's wrong,' she said, staring right into me as if she had a right to know. 'Your studies are suffering. I'm hearing all sorts of rumours about you and about this band and recording studios and all kinds of nonsense. What's going on, Amy?'

'It's nothing to do with the band,' I said.

'What's the band called?' she said.

I hesitated. 'Car Crime.'

She paused. 'Amy,' she said, 'why do you think the band's called that? Did Ben choose the name?'

'Yes,' I said.

'Why, do you think? Did anybody else have a say in it? I mean, what do you know about his reasons for –'

'It's my parents!' I said, quite truthfully.

'Your parents?'

'My dad lost his job. He can't cope. My mum's had to go back out to work. I've got two little twin sisters. I have to help my dad. He can't manage without me. It's our house. It's going completely mad.'

✱✱✱ Thirteen

The truth was, our house *was* going mad; and getting madder by the day. My dad seemed to be managing the twins by dipping their hands in washing up liquid and then letting them loose round the house collecting as much house dust and detritus as possible.

'Thank God!' he'd bellow, as soon as I walked through the door. 'Amy!' he'd roar. 'Quick! See if you can mop some of that water off the kitchen floor. Don't bother to talk to me, I've stopped listening to anything. I think my ears have turned to play dough.'

The kitchen was covered in blackened bits, as if an evil experiment had gone ever so badly wrong.

'See if you can scrape some of the black off those pots on the cooker, will you?' he dashed by with a plastic bin liner, with a hole cut out of it, draped over his body.

'Dad,' I asked 'what is –'

'That's my tie,' he dashed by saying, as I flicked the charred embers from the gas rings. 'I don't need it,' he happily exclaimed, as if he really was glad to lose it. But: 'My best tie,' he'd almost immediately lament, his moods swinging like a millisecond manic-depressive.

Whenever I was late home from rehearsals with the band, I'd find him face down on the living room floor in a near catatonic daze with the twins riding his head. What looked like cat's hair in between their fingers and over the carpet had once belonged to my dad.

I never told Dad about the A and R man at Solar. I never told my mum, either. I couldn't tell either of them. He'd be too harassed by then; and she'd be coming home late again expecting no dinner, nor getting any.

'You get fed at school,' my dad would say, 'at lunchtimes, don't you?'

'Just as well I do,' she'd say, spreading the empty dining table with books to mark and whole heaps of National Curriculum reporting forms to fill in. 'Look at this lot,' she'd say. 'I'd forgotten what's been happening to teachers. No wonder so many of us choose to do other things.'

'Like staying at home to look after their kids properly,' my dad would say, getting another dig in as often as he could.

'Or going out doing any one of the thousand other things teachers are good at,' she'd return, each batting their caustic comments at one another as if in a game of very vindictive tennis.

'Like not looking after their families,' he'd bat with.

'Or like being the only one in the household capable of making any money at all,' she'd backhand her return, each parry gathering speed and spite.

I had to come out of the way every time, before they'd rope me in like an unwilling umpire. I couldn't stand it. They were like two people I'd never met before, the sort of people that made you cringe, bickering and barking in the street at their wayward and grubby little kids.

I didn't tell them a thing. We went for the Solar Records audition when we should have been at school, with parental permission for everyone but me. Kirsten's mum and dad had invested what must have been a small fortune in a new designer outfit for the most beautiful and alluring young star in the whole of Wannabe Wonderland. Beccs/Becky turned up in her football kit but with a short skirt. Geoff's mum came with him and only left when he begged her with tears in his eyes and we three girls assured her we would be looking after him at all times. Ben got dropped off in another too-nice motor driven by another too-young stranger. While I truanted on the bus with my out-of-school jeans and tee shirt and trainers stuffed into my rucksack.

We met up with about three hours to go, spent an hour reassuring Geoff's mum, kicked around for an hour and turned up an hour early at the studios. We were keyed up and over-excited, expecting the A and R man to be eagerly awaiting our arrival on the strength of our demo tape, with a cigar in one hand and a recording contract in the other. We turned up an hour early; they didn't know who we were.

Eventually they found us way down on a long, long list, listed as The Car Keys. The man on the door told us where to go. There was nobody there. We had to wait. We had to wait a long, long, long, long time.

Another bunch of old bald guys in black tee shirts and pony tails finally turned up and told us where to go to wait. We had to wait a long, long, long, long time.

'This is normal,' Ben kept telling us.

We waited. A long, long, long, long – anyway, we got hungry. Starving hungry. We had to shoot out for a burger, stuffing it down on the way back.

'You've missed your slot,' one of the ponytails told us on our return. 'You'll have to wait.'

We waited. We waited. And we waited. A long, long, extra etcetera time.

Afterwards, we crept home quietly, saying goodbye to each other as if we all had a secret to keep. In a way, we did. We'd made a complete mess of it. Nothing went right. We were hopeless, worse than a bunch of tired Grunge Machine mechanics, but we couldn't ever tell anyone. Without speaking about it, we agreed we would not speak about it. We snuck home on the quiet, playing it down, ignoring the fact that we'd come over like another bunch of weekend wannabes. Which is what we were.

They'd let us do none of our rehearsed stuff. They, Solar Records, seemed to have got us there on false pretences. The A and R man might have listened to our tape, who knows? If we saw an A and R man that day, we never knew it. There seemed to be an abundance of sound technicians and big-bellied ex-roadies lounging over coffee and cigarettes. There was a girl with a clipboard and little headphones and a mike, telling everyone where to go, directing the proceedings according to – according to nothing, apparently. The day was an absolute shambles. They still had us on their list as The Car Keys, with no idea what we were supposed to sound like. There was no sign of our tape, or anyone that seemed to know anything about us.

They got us trying to harmonise cover versions of old chart songs, pop ballads we all, but especially Ben, hated. They asked us lots of questions that didn't seem to have anything to do with anything.

'Who plays lead guitar?' the clipboard girl asked, looking down her nose at Geoffrey.

Geoff looked to Ben for help. 'We're not a guitar band,' Ben said.

'Are any of you girls Irish?' the clipboard girl asked, ticking the different and equally irrelevant things off her list.

They made us mess up a couple of very ordinary pop tunes

111

already messed up in the charts by the girlie girl bands Kirsten would have most liked to be in. Geoff had to try some keyboard things on his own on a strange keyboard, from which he almost died of embarrassment. Ben couldn't make contact with anyone, as much as he tried to win over the clipboard girl. He was powerless. We all were.

We slunk away late in the evening with our tails between our legs and said an almost silent goodbye to each other. We were like the losers in a fight. We didn't want to talk about it. We especially didn't want to have to talk to anybody else about it.

I felt drained, physically and mentally. My head was full of cotton wool and a vague, thickening ache. It felt as if sometime, sometime fairly soon, I might even consider being sick.

'Where have you been!' my mother yelled when I arrived home to a silent house. Silent, that is, but for the shouting voice of my mother.

'Where have you been!'

My dad sat like another guilty party at one end of the settee. The house looked as close as it ever came to tidy. My dad had on clean clothes; the few stains on his chin and rapidly rising forehead may or may not have been bruises. Some of his hair was missing. He looked very red.

'You haven't been to school, have you!'

I'd got changed again on the way home, thinking that my mother wouldn't be here yet, and that my dad never even knew what day of the week it was, so he'd have no chance of knowing if I'd been to rehearsals or not. I came in wearing my school stuff like I was trying to fool everybody. Like, I was fooling nobody.

'You haven't been to school! Where have you been?'

I glanced dizzily at my dad.

'Don't go looking to him for support. He hasn't got a clue what's going on. You haven't been to school, I know you haven't.'

'We had a phone call,' my dad said.

'Oh,' I said, swallowing hard. My head was banging, echoing with words and anger.

'Yes,' my mum snapped, 'Oh. Oh dear. It's all wrong, isn't it, Amy? This band, taking days off school, your studies going down the drain. What did you think you were doing?'

'It isn't like that,' I said, trying hard to focus on something.

'Oh,' she said. 'Then maybe you'd better tell us what it *is* like. You better tell us what it's like, throwing your future away before you've even got started. I couldn't believe it, the things I was hearing. Your maths, your physics, *and* your biology. After all the work we've done together, you want to throw it away for some silly – some stupid, stupid singing group without even –'

'Mum!' I had to try not to scream. 'I've tried – I've tried and tried to ask you to help me. But you're always –'

'When? When have you?'

'All the time, Mum. It hasn't worked. It's nothing to do with the band.'

'I told you so,' my dad only went and said.

'Oh yes!' she turned on him, shouting down at him, shouting him down. 'You told me so. Of course you told me so. What else would you have possibly said but that it's my fault?'

'It isn't –' I tried to say.

'Well it isn't mine,' he said, smugly, but loud enough to drown me out. 'It isn't mine, for a change, that's for sure.'

'What's the matter with you?' she was shrieking at him. 'It's always got to be somebody's fault with you, hasn't it?'

'Oh. Not with you then?'

'No. Not with me. All right? Not with me!'

'No? That's not how it feels to me.'

'I don't care how it feels to you. *She's* the important one!' my mum shrieked, pointing at me.

I was too tired. I'd drunk too much coffee or coke or something. I'd been too excited, then too disappointed. I couldn't remember if I'd taken my tablets. My head was crashing. There were little squirms of darkness in the corners of my eyes as the twins started to scream a double protest from upstairs and my parents' shrieks amalgamated into one single roar under the too-bright living room light. I felt my bag fall to the floor. The room started to shift. The light slid by me as my legs went and the floor came up to meet me as I fought like crazy against everything that was crowding into me.

✳✳✳ Fourteen

I had to miss the next day at school after such a nasty epileptic fit. There was no remembering it, of course, but I had a fair few bruises on my arms and legs and on my back to show just how fit the fit had been. If you've never had a fit or seizure yourself, and I hope you haven't and never will, you won't know what it's like. You cannot know what having a seizure is like, because even us people that have them do not know what it is like to have one. We're out of it by then. The bit you see as a spectator, the gnashing and thrashing bit, is unknown to the person gnashing and thrashing on the floor. All we know of it is the peppery confusion of a sick headache, a confusion of heat and light beforehand, and the recovery after. The bit in between's a mystery to everyone.

But I knew this had been a particularly bad one by the level of fatigue I had afterwards. I'd put a lot into it; I had quite a lot of recovering to do. I'd come round surrounded by the coats and cushions my mum and dad had tried to shield me with. There wasn't any knowing what had happened for a while. All I felt was an ache and a tiredness. The ache was everywhere, absolutely everywhere. Every muscle in my body had been over-tensed too suddenly, the tiredness a total fatigue of body and brain.

'You're okay,' my mum was saying to me, over and over as I came round. 'Take these,' she said, giving me my anti-epilepsy medication.

They had to put me to bed to sleep off the aftermath. But the thing, or the hidden section in my brain, the epileptic cells were still popping, giving me a light display of colour in the darkness with my eyes tightly closed. A shallow, unsatisfying sleep weaved its way in and out of the epileptic nerve shudderings as my eyes wouldn't settle under the coloured light, and my hands and feet felt full of a sporadic electrical energy that had me tensing and flipping from one side to the other all night. Come morning, I was fit for nothing, without the mind to care, one way or the other. The fiasco at Solar Records had dampened my spirits, while my mother had frightened me into realising, only too clearly, the completeness of my failure.

She took the morning away from her work, my mum; to be sure that I was all right, she told me and my dad and her school. But I knew she wanted to talk to me to find out how far the rot had set in.

'Have I really been so very bad at helping you?' she said, perched on the side of my bed.

She felt as if she'd let me down, I could tell. But I felt as if I'd let the band down. I still felt dizzy with bad food and failure from yesterday, wondering what Ben was feeling, and if it was the same as me.

'You've had too much against you,' I said, to try to make at least my mum feel a bit better.

She smiled. 'We'll put it right,' she said, confidently.

That was, of course, before we got out my exercise books and she came to realise just how very far behind I'd let myself become. It was awful, horrible to have to admit how stupid her daughter, the daughter in whom she'd taken so much pride, could be. I felt stupid; as I had the day before, singing girl-group songs at the top and bottom of my voice while Kirsten and Becky went through some of the old pop routines

116

they'd rehearsed, while Geoffrey shrink-wrapped himself in self-consciousness and Ben blew it out in disgust.

I felt stupid. My mum's confidence waned rapidly as I demonstrated for her quite clearly how stupid I had become. 'We'll just have to put the hours in together,' she said. 'Every night, right? And I mean, every night.'

Meaning, of course, that the rehearsals, the two evenings a week round Geoff's would have to stop. Which they would; I'd have to go to school now as if I was going to school, to do what we did at school, like everybody else. It was like a lesson in not being special. I was just like everybody else. The quicker I came to terms with that fact, the better off I'd be.

So I went back to school the next day, like everybody else. Beccs was there, without Kirsty. Kirsty was off sick, Beccs told me.

'I wasn't well yesterday, either,' I told her. 'I had a fit the day before. A bad one.'

'Yeah,' she said. 'I think we all did.'

She went off, without a mention of the band. I watched her walk away. Car Crime had crashed, badly. So badly, that Geoff couldn't bring himself to even talk to me. I saw him, but he veered away, like his long mother, sloping round a corner as soon as he caught sight of me. I let him go. I was at school; that was all there was to it. School was it, from now on.

But Geoff came back, having apparently changed his mind. He caught up with me in the corridor. 'I d-d-d-d-'

'Geoff,' I said, 'take more time.'

'I d-don't know wh-what to d-d-do,' he said. He was reddening as he spoke, looking down at me. 'T-t-tell me wh-what to do, Amy.'

'What can I tell you about, Geoff?' I said.

'About K-k – about Kirsty,' he said. Some people were moving round us. Geoff looked as if he was about to cry.

117

'Look,' I said, 'come in here,' leading him into an empty classroom. 'Geoff, it's okay. What's wrong?'

'I d-d-d-'

'Geoff,' I said, 'take more time to speak. Breathe properly. Come on. It's okay. Tell me.'

He breathed, red in the face, blinking quickly. 'I – I d-don't know – it's – I d-don't know wh-what to d-do. She's – I'm, like, all over the place. She – wh-why d-did she – kiss me, like that? I-i-in front of the wh-whole school? Wh-why d-d-do that – if sh-she was only g-going to treat me – treat me like this? I d-don't get it? I d-d-d-'

He stopped, blinking down at me. 'Geoff,' I said, looking up into his face, 'what can I tell you?'

Well, what could I tell him? The truth? I don't think so. The truth could have only hurt him still further, and he was hurting quite enough as it was.

'Y-you c-c-can tell me wh-what to do,' he said.

'There's nothing you can do,' I told him. 'That's what she's like. She just does things. They might mean something to you, they don't to her.'

He was looking down at me, his soft face falling.

'Come here,' I told him, holding out my arms to hug him. I only came up to about his waist, but hung on until he'd almost stopped crying. Yes, he was crying. I could feel the little shudders of it.

Some loud louts were kicking by outside the room, clouting the door on their way past. Geoff covered his face with his hand. I looked up to see Peter Stevens peering through the glass panel of the door. I pulled Geoffrey further round the corner, where they wouldn't be able to see that he was crying. We stayed together like that until I could feel him breathing more regularly.

'I've got to go,' I said. 'I'm going to be late.'

'And m-me,' he said.

I looked up at him: he, down, way down at me. He bent towards me so that I could kiss him. I kissed him on the cheek. 'Speak to Ben,' I said.

'N-no one knows wh-where he is,' Geoff said. 'He hasn't b-b-been a-around. His m-mobile's off – all the t-time. I called his house. His m-mum s-s-said he's a-a-at school.'

'And he isn't?'

'N-no, he isn't. I c-can't f-f-f-find him. He g-goes all over th-the – the place. He's like – he's everywhere, in c-cars, all over th-th-the –'

'In cars?' I said, urgently. 'Whose cars are they?'

Geoffrey shrugged.

'What do you know about it, Geoff? Tell me.'

Geoffrey shrugged again, reddening.

'You know he's out and about in cars. How do you know that, Geoff? Tell me. You've been out with him, is that it?'

'I've g-g-got to g-go,' he said, shifting away from me.

'Geoff, don't go. Geoff! That's not right for you, don't you know that?' I found myself calling after him. He was hurrying out of the empty classroom into the corridor. 'You're not like that,' I was calling, as Geoffrey was hurrying by the grunge-sters lolling at the foot of the stairs.

'You're not like that, Geoff. Neither is he, really. You tell him that, if you see him. Tell him I said he's an idiot. He's an idiot!' I was shouting, as Stevens and Bradshaw started to smile at each other.

I had to go straight home that evening. It was Friday, the weekend. Crazy, how everything could change so quickly, in the space of one school week. Car Crime had crashed. Every-

119

one was wandering away alone. Ben's mobile was switched off.

'You go without leaving Ben Lyons a message,' his message said, 'and I'll never call you back.'

I didn't leave a message. I felt like screaming into the telephone: 'Why are you doing this to me?' I called his number again; again, his voice message. 'Call me,' I said, quietly. 'Ben, call me.'

When I got home, my dad was performing miracles in the kitchen. There were things actually in the oven, cooking. *Cooking*, of all things. My dad's hair had been washed and looked almost in one piece. He was relatively clean, which was not clean at all, but relatively. So were the twins. He had them sitting in their high chairs on opposite sides of the table. I couldn't see any egg or blood or beans or offal climbing down the walls. There were no terrorised stray cats under the table or dead ravens in blackened pots on the stove.

'What's happening?' I said, nervously, my back pressed against the wall. There was just too much silence all at once, too much innocence on the happy faces of my sunny sisters. 'What's the matter with those two?' I said.

'Hello, Amy,' my dad said, his relaxed face also smiling. 'What two? Georgie and Jo? They're okay. What do you mean?'

'What's happened to the house?' I said, looking everywhere for breakages, melted glass, masticated wall-plaster.

'The house? It's all right, isn't it? It should be, we've been out most of the day, haven't we girls?' The girls kicked their little legs in their clean high chairs. 'It's quite good fun, actually. We walked all over the place. We went to the park, didn't we, girls?'

The girls kicked and gurgled, but half-heartedly. I could see now what it was, they were tired out.

'I think we're all going to get a good night's sleep tonight, aren't we, girls?'

The girls blinked, softly.

'Your mum's on her way home,' my dad said. 'She wants to have a look at your homework with you. And there's a –'

The telephone started ringing.

'That'll be the phone,' my dad said. He always, but always said that whenever the telephone rang. 'You get it. It'll probably be for you. There's a message left for you, too.'

'Hello?' I said, closing the kitchen door as I picked up the telephone receiver.

'What are we going to do?'

'Ben!' I said. 'Why haven't you called me? Where are you?'

'Out and about,' he said. 'What do you think? Are we going to let it go?'

'Let it go? Like you're letting school go? Like that?'

'Forget about that.'

'Maybe you can. I'm not like you.'

'Oh, you are, Amy. A lot like me. You know that, don't you.'

I didn't say anything. I didn't have to.

'It's just a set-back,' Ben said. 'We weren't prepared properly. We need more experience. I can get us a few gigs in a few clubs. I know a few people.'

'I know you do.'

'You have to know people, you know?'

'I know. But it isn't just that. It – I've let it get in the way. I'm in trouble at school now and –'

'Well join the club!'

'No, Ben. I don't want to be in that club. It isn't right for me.'

'Neither am I then, eh?'

'No, don't – I didn't mean that.'

121

'Well, I didn't get much of a response, when I tried to get a kiss.'

'No, that's not fair. We were here, standing in my hall at home. It wasn't right for me. It was, but not here. The timing was all wrong.'

'That's what I'm trying to say about Car Crime. The timing was wrong, that's all. That's all. It's good, Amy, you know it. *We're* good. It works, you can feel it. I know you can. I've seen you.'

We went silent. He'd seen me. Yes, I knew he had. We'd looked at each other. It *was* good. We were. It worked, I could feel it.

'You don't want to let it go,' Ben said, 'as much as I don't.'

'I can't make rehearsals during the week,' I said. 'I have to concentrate on school.'

'Weekends then,' he said. 'This weekend. Tomorrow, round Geoff's. I'll see you there. Two o'clock. Okay? I'll call Geoff. You tell Kirsty and Beccs, yeah? What do you say? Tomorrow, two o'clock?'

I put down the receiver. What was so troublesome about being in a band? It should have been simple, shouldn't it? Shouldn't we have been just a bunch of kids messing about, making a racket no one but ourselves could call music? What was there that was so – so destructive? Car Crime? Destructive enough in itself, especially as the actuality of racing the ring road round the town at a ton, ton-twenty in stolen cars happened regularly, only just out of earshot of my home and school.

I'd be there, at two o'clock tomorrow round Geoff's; what choice did I have? On the one hand I had my A-levels, on the other Car Crime and Ben. When Ben looked at me, whenever he looked at me, there was no hand other than the one that included Car Crime, and him.

Besides, I'd been messing up my studies on my own quite effectively, without the assistance of any car criminals. My mum was on her way home early from work to try to help me; but she couldn't, she just couldn't. So what would be the use of abandoning the band, of giving up on Ben right now, just when things between us were getting – well, as if there were things, good things, between us.

'Did you pick up your message?' my dad asked, as I appeared back in the kitchen.

'No,' I said, 'I forgot.'

I went back to the telephone, leaving the kitchen door open behind me. I could see Dad giving the girls soldiers of buttered bread for their tea. I dialled the messaging service. One message: received today, at three-thirty.

My dad looked from the kitchen to the hall at me, as the message from three-thirty this afternoon clicked in, saying: 'Hello? This is Raymond Raymond. I'm from Solar Records. I'm, ah, calling to leave a message. Message for Amy Peppercorn – great name! Yes. Amy, there's a little, ah, project I'm working on. You might be interested. Call me. Mobile. Here's the number . . . That's it. Thanks. Bye.'

Then gone.

I looked up to find my dad looking at me with a bowl in his hands over the waste-bin as I stood there with my mouth hanging open. The twins were watching me, too, their three faces like a triangle of moons in the kitchen. 'Do you know,' my dad said, as I stood there stunned, 'how difficult it is to get rid of couscous?'

✳✳✳ Fifteen

Wednesday evening, and I was pretending to be coming home from school again. I wasn't coming home from school: in my bag, my jeans and tee shirt and trainers. No text books. No maths. No physics or biology. I was in danger of forgetting completely what each of those subjects was about. As it was, they seemed to exist in my memory and my imagination as one amorphous blob of unknowing. Whenever I thought about them, which was often and always with dread, I wondered how there could be certain things in the world that were either mathematical, or biological, or they were not. Very strange. And were things to do with physics, physical? Even stranger.

That's what I was to my chosen topics of study: a complete stranger. I felt outside of understanding, excluded from it. Actually, I felt outside of almost everything. The phone call did it. My dad had looked at me strangely, like a stranger looking at a stranger, but had asked me about chucking couscous into the bin. I didn't say anything to him.

'What's up?' he said, as I seemed to gag for breath.

I almost told him, then chose to say nothing. 'Nothing,' I said. I could have not said nothing, I suppose; I did have the choice. But I chose to say nothing until I'd called the A and R man at Solar to hear what it was he had to say to me.

I suppose I could have not said nothing to the others at the Car Crime rehearsal on Saturday, either. When Ben was winding up his enthusiasm, telling us all what he'd told me over the phone the day before, I could have told them that the A and R man at Solar wanted to see me, just me, on Wednesday, because he had a song that might suit me and he had some dancers for the day and would I like to try the song out to see how it sounds and how we'd look on pre-production video? Would I like to? What could I have told them?

Wednesday evening, and I was pretending to be coming home from school again. I wasn't coming home from school; I was returning confused from Solar Records where the A and R man had received me in person and shaken me by the hand and asked me what my real name was.

'Amy Peppercorn,' I said.

'Fantastic!' he gushed. 'Love it! Couldn't be better. Come in, Amy Peppercorn, come in. Let me tell you – let me tell you, you have a voice. A voice, Amy Peppercorn. How tall would you be?'

'I'd be a good two metres,' I said.

He laughed. 'Fair enough. Feisty little package, eh? Good. Got your own mind. Am I right? Am I right? Ray Ray,' he said, holding out his hand.

His name really was Raymond Raymond. I shook Ray Ray's hand as if I was as cool as the dead and just as uncaring: which, perhaps, I was. This wasn't right. I was a member of Car Crime. We were good together. I didn't want to be here without the others. Without Beccs. Without Ben. I didn't want to do this without Ben smiling at me, without that look between us that sent those shivers of anticipation up my spine.

Ray Ray, the A and R man for Solar, took me through to the studios. Not the claustrophobic closets we were encased in last week, but a proper recording suite with some kind of a production set outside with cameras and something like thirty or forty people hanging round drinking coffee and eating doughnuts. They looked up and looked round at me as I appeared at the glass side of the studio with Ray Ray.

'Are they all –' I said, without knowing what it was that I was about to say. They were all looking at me, as if I was something for them all to look at. 'So many people,' I said. I felt nervous for the first time. I hadn't really wanted to come here, thinking that I was going to insist that all I was, was a member of Car Crime, and that was all there was to it. But the whole cast and crew of some movie set were looking at me expectantly, as if – as if I was what they were all doing here.

Ray was laughing. 'You'll get used to it,' he said.

I looked at him. 'Will I?'

He smiled. 'Great voice,' he said. 'Listen – this song. Got to be right for that voice. We know, you know? You come over really well. Wendy told me. Singing, moving. Confidence, yeah?'

'Wendy?'

'Last week? Wendy?' he said, pointing to the clipboard girl, who waved from the other side of the studio.

'Oh,' I said, waving back. 'Wendy. Right.'

'Yeah. She said – you know, your mates? Your friends, all that. Sorry, but this is business. Only a few make it, yeah? Only a very, very – yeah? Know what I'm saying?'

'Yes.'

'One of the few? Amy Peppercorn? The way you sound, your looks –'

'My looks?'

'Yeah – yeah? I mean, don't underestimate – right costume – right make-up – right surroundings. Right song. Could be – you *could* be one of the few. Little Amy Peppercorn, yeah? Could be on your way.'

Now I was on my way home, pretending to be coming from

school. I was thirsty, hungry, tired, confused. My hair smelled of cigarette smoke and electricity. My face still showed a few smudges of the studio's over-the-top make-up. One of my eyes kept sticking together. My legs ached from stomping through the dance routines thirty or forty times too many. My head was full of song-lyrics learned by rote and repeated over and over with so many changes to tune and dramatic emphasis:

> *The word is out there*
>   *The word on the street*
> *There is no doubt there*
>   *Is a life so incomplete*
> *When you're not about where*
>   *We always used to meet*
> *But now the word is on the street*
>   *My love, you're back*
> *And our love's back on the right track*
>   *Now the word is on the street.*

It was called *The Word on the Street*, of course. All it did was to repeat the same few lines, again and again, with an instrumental bit in between. Two old guys had written it. They were there in the crowd at the studio. They must have been nearly my dad's age. Apparently, they'd written hundreds of hit songs, in the past. I don't know. It was like – too much like Kirsty; too cutesy and sweet for my taste, too girl-band, especially with me and six other little girlie-girls all in a V formation on the stage stamping out these little dance routines they'd devised. It wasn't anything you hadn't seen done a thousand times before, with all those little hackneyed moves, and little Amy Peppercorn wearing too much make-up, supposed to be sultry and yearning and desirable, looking out the corner of my eye at the camera.

'More lip!' someone from over one side kept calling out to me. 'More lip!'

Meaning that I was supposed to do this kind of Kirsty-pout they wanted for the close-ups at the ends of every little routine. And the routines were little. They lasted never more than a couple of seconds at a time. We didn't have to do much, really. But it was me and all my little girlfriends doing our teen-dance on a stage all wearing very similar, but not exactly the same outfits. Too cutesy!

Ordinarily, ordinarily I would have felt like puking. Beccs and I always made out to stick our fingers down our throats whenever we saw the girlie girls-in-a-vee dance routines on the music television channels. Or we did before the advent of Kirsten, in whose opinion the Oops! routines were just the very thing. Or we did before all these people at Solar made it all seem so very wonderful and clever and exciting and new when I did it, dancing at the front of my very own vee-formation, miming the words to my very own pre-recorded version of my very own pre-production pop song.

I succumbed to the flattery of the applause and the jealous admiration of the other girl dancers. I was the very centre of attention of all the production crew and A and R personnel in practically the whole of Solar Records. It felt like nothing I'd ever experienced. Even when we stopped for a brought-in burger lunch I was given pride of place, treated as if I was really special, and set to become more special still.

At the end of the day, Ray Ray had me sitting in his office upstairs surrounded by gold and silver records and signed photographs of the old rockers my dad liked. 'The girl done good,' he was saying to me. 'Now we have to – all too much – wind and water – justifications, to the board, yeah? Haven't got a clue, most of 'em. Still, all have to have their say. Half of them, they think we're looking for new Bob Dylans, yeah?' he said, laughing.

I squeezed a smile.

'No. You haven't – heard of? I suppose?'

'No,' I said. 'Do I need to know?'

'No! Absolutely, no,' he said, laughing again. 'No, seriously. We have to do – it's such a load of crap. Budget projections, etc, etc. You don't need to know that, either. Wish I didn't.'

'So what do I do next?'

'Go home. We'll, you know, be in touch, yeah? We've got a car, if you like. Take you home? Driver?'

'Can I take the bus?' I said. I had to look as if I was coming home from school. I had to get my head right, to come down to street level, to go back to worrying about my A-levels and my crazy home life, and to Car Crime.

Ray Ray laughed again, offering me my bus fare. I didn't take it. I took the bus, but not the fare, trying to pull myself together.

My mum was going to tear me apart.

'You haven't been to school again! I know you haven't been to school again! And don't you dare throw another fit! I want to know where you've been! I demand to know where you've been! Because if it's anything to do with that other thing –'

'Let her tell you where she's been,' my father interjected, holding the twins upside down. They seemed fascinated at how everything looked from that way up.

I had to tell them, all of them, where I'd been and what I'd been doing.

'What about your studies?' my mum said.

'What about Car Crime?' Beccs said, when I told her the next day.

'Never mind about Car Crime,' my dad said, when I told him what Beccs had said that day. 'Never mind about that. You've had another call, today. They're not wasting any time. You're to go back to the studios next week. They think they're going ahead. They want you, Amy.'

'Of all the crafty little cows!' Kirsten said. Well, she would, wouldn't she? But she and Beccs were wearing a very similar expression as she said it.

'You're too far behind at school as it is,' my mother said.

'You must be joking!' my father cried. 'This is the chance of a lifetime.'

'The chance of a lifetime,' Ben said, but looking at me as if my lifetime was happening at another time and in another place to his own.

'Why didn't you tell me?' Beccs said.

'Why didn't you tell me?' asked Ben.

'Why didn't you tell us?' – my mother.

'Why d-did you tell K-Kirsty to kiss me i-i-i-in front of the whole school, then mmm-m-make out it was all her?' Geoffrey came and accused me.

'Why were you kissing Geoff in that empty classroom the other day?' Ben wanted to know.

'Why don't you get lost?' Kirsten was kind enough to ask.

'Why didn't you tell me?' – Beccs again; hurt, very hurt.

'Why d-did you have to get K-K-Kirsty to do that t-t-to me?' – Geoff, very, very hurt.

'Why kiss Geoff like that, in front of Stevens and that lot?' – Ben, indignant.

'Why?' – Beccs, because I couldn't answer her. I could have lied, but didn't. So I couldn't answer her.

'Why do they need three days next week?' – my mother.

'What does it matter?' – my father to my mother. 'This is the chance of a lifetime. What does another three days away from school matter?'

'Why don't you care about her education?' – my mother to my father.

'Why don't you give her a chance to take the opportunity of a lifetime? This could be good for us all, couldn't it?'

'Could be good for you, you mean, don't you?'

'What do you mean by that?'

'Don't you know?'

'Why don't you tell me?'

'Why don't you shut up for a while?'

'Why don't you?'

'Why don't you care about your daughter's future?'

'Why don't you?'

'Why don't you get lost?' – Kirsten, at every possible opportunity.

'Why?' – my best friend, Beccs. 'Why?'

'Why don't you face it, Lyons,' – Peter Stevens, leader of the New Grunge, 'she's made you look like a right tosser, hasn't she?'

'Why do you think you can use people like you do?' – just about everyone!

*** Sixteen

What do you mean?' – Raymond Raymond, A and R, Solar Records, the very next week.

I was going to be there for three days. They'd done the business justifications, apparently, in record time. Solar Records only ever did things in record time. When they made their minds up, Solar burned with the heat and intensity of the sun.

We were going for it. Ray, the very sun's bright light, told me I was a Solar star in the making; so get down to the studios quickly for the make-over, the hair, the lipgloss, on with the false lashes again, the right clothes and the eternal sound and lighting tests. 'The sun shines bright down at Solar,' Ray shone, his artists and his repertoire gathering and expanding around him.

But an entire week of questions I could or could not answer had ditched me dumbfounded and shaking, my confidence dragged from under me as I tried to dance, tripping me over onto my bum in front of the shining happy people of Solar.

'Okay, okay,' Ray Ray was stepping forward saying, putting everyone back into their starting positions as I sat stupid on my short rump. 'Something wrong, Amy? Last week, good. This, bad. What's happened? You all right?'

'Yes,' I said. My short hair had been spiked. I had enough make-up on to disguise myself from my mother. My clothes were too tight. 'Yes,' I said, 'I'm all right. I'm just – I'm tired. I haven't been sleeping properly.'

'You want to take a break? Can we take a break? Short one?' he turned and said to the production manager.

We'd been putting the song down, going over and over and over it. I knew and hated the words with all my heart.

'Fifteen minutes!' the production manager shouted to everybody.

'I know,' Ray came and said, sitting down next to me, 'yeah. I know, what it's like. The initial excitement. Then the hard slog. Putting it all together. It don't go. You know? Don't worry. Keep going. Tomorrow night, all be over. You're doing great. Don't worry.'

But I was worried. I was worried about the reaction of all my friends and family to what was happening. I was worried by being seen to be such a hypocrite. The song was just everything I'd always made such a big thing of despising. It was teen-angst, boy-ridden and written for Kirsten and her Girl Fridays out in the shopping mall imagining themselves making their own vee-formation pop video there, with everybody watching. I'd always been publicly and loudly against that image, accusing them of following in their vees like gaggles of geese across the sky with no option but to conform.

This was exactly what we were creating here; or re-creating, for the nth time, because it had all been done in the past. And I was the newest raw recruit, looking out from the front of the vee fresh faced, with my hair spiked and my made-over face like a mask and my clothes too tight for a girl with my tastes.

'No, seriously,' Ray Ray was saying. 'If there is – something wrong, you know. If there's anything – I can do?' He was leaning forward to look into my face. He could see I wasn't

133

enjoying myself here at Solar, now that we were supposed to be doing it all for real.

'It's my mum,' I said.

'Ah,' he said, leaning back. 'Ah.' He knew that she had deep, deep reservations about what we were doing. 'Your mum,' he said.

'Yes,' I said. 'She's worried.'

'What's to worry her? I don't – what can I do? Stop her worrying? Eh?'

'Well, if you could teach me the differential coefficients of trigonometrical functions, it'd be a great help.'

My mum had been coming home early from work, bringing great piles of books with her, to do my maths work with me. 'Look,' she'd been saying, 'look, here. It's as simple as this. The differential of sine x is cosine x because if you draw a sine wave like this, see for yourself how its rate of change is zero at its maximum and maximum as it crosses the zero line. If you compare what you have to a cosine wave, you'll see it's exactly the same. See? See?'

She'd thrown a pencil across the room in the end. I couldn't see a thing. My pictures were all gone from me. Instead, all I was were the feelings, the emotions of coping with everyone's questions:

'Why didn't you tell me?'

'Why don't you get lost?'

'Why did you let that happen?'

'Why did you let it happen like that?'

Until I was dizzy with not knowing what I'd done or why. I could hardly remember anything. Learning something new was out of the question. My mother threw a pencil across the room in frustration. She was not the teacher she had once been, because I was not the same pupil.

My father had caught the pencil in the back of his head,

which made absolutely no difference to him; he was being bombarded by spaghetti and Lego at the time, so felt nothing.

'Can't you keep the girls quiet for a few minutes?' my mother had yelled.

'How am I supposed to teach anybody anything?'

'If you could teach me differential calculus,' I found myself saying to Ray Ray, 'it'd be a great help.'

'Would it?' he said. 'That make you feel good, would it? Half the population would kill to be you – in your shoes. That thing, differwhatsname thingy, whatever it is, would really make you feel good, would it?'

I thought about it. I thought about my friends in Car Crime, the family scream I'd inherited that I wasn't allowed to use at Solar Records. 'Well,' I said, 'perhaps it'd help if I actually liked *The Word On The Street*.'

Ray faltered, his sunlight dimming for a few moments. 'What do you mean?' he smiled.

'The song,' I said. 'I don't like it.'

'You don't like it?'

I shook my head against his smile.

'You don't like the song?'

'Or what we're doing here. Or this,' I said, waving my hand across the film set behind me, 'this girlie dance routine stuff. All this. It isn't me. That isn't what I wanted to do.'

'Isn't it?' he smiled. 'What was it you wanted to do, might I ask? – No, listen, Amy Peppercorn. This is a business, right? – No, listen. I said listen. You don't need to answer if I ask you something. Right? – Good. This business – the music business, is *the* business. You understand? You either succeed or you don't. The business doesn't make any concessions for you. Or your friends. Or your particular tastes. Or preferences. It either sells, or it doesn't. We know what sells. *I*

135

know what sells. There's a pulse. My finger's on it. There's a pulse but there's no heart. If you wanna do this, fine. If not, there's a hundred – no, a hundred thousand queuing at my door. Queuing up. For half a chance. You can sing, Amy Peppercorn. But so can hundreds of others.

'Now. You might not make it yet, there's no knowing. Some people's faces just don't fit. Know what I mean? I mean, they just don't have that spark. That quality. I haven't made up my mind about you yet. Not yet. Nobody has. You still got a lot of persuading to do.

'You think cutting this record and taping this vid's it, don't you? – Let me tell you something. We do this sort of thing all the time. *All the time!* Most of it comes to nothing.

'It's an investment we have to make. We're doing our part. You can do yours. Or you can go and do something else. You can go and play pop stars with your mates. You can worry about your mum and dad. You can get your exams and go work in the local bank. Or you can sing this song – *this song* – and dance your little butt off. And enjoy it. The choice is yours.

'We don't have time to prat about. We don't have room for no mousy schoolgirls. Know what I mean? Know what I mean? I mean, you with me, Amy Peppercorn, or not? You can answer.'

'Yes,' I said.

'Good,' he said. 'Now you got, what – four minutes? Make up your mind. Either get up or get out. It's all the same to me.'

I was up in three. Calculus was not now an option. I'd blown that one. This had to be it, the thing I was going to do above my exams and my family and my – my friends would understand. Of anybody in the world, surely my friends would be with me? Which of them wouldn't jump at a chance like this?

I had to remind myself that I was making a pop video, singing the lead, for a major recording studio with the clout to sell this thing. Then the next thing, and the next. Until . . . until whatever. I was doing it, wasn't I? Every young person's dream? Every not-so-young person's dream, and here I was on the road to my flicker of fame and hopefully substantial fortune.

Besides, we needed the money . . .

Besides, my dad wanted me to do it . . .

Besides, I'd be stupid not to . . .

Besides, I was really good at this . . .

I could sing!

I did sing.

I could dance!

I did! You just watch the video. We looked good. Unoriginal, yes: but good. Better than most. Better than – ah, but you know who I'm better than. *She* knows it, too. I don't need to tell you. *She* knows who I mean; *she's* had, what, four hit singles, and she's not worth a – I'm far and away more talented than Courtney Schaeffer. If she can do it . . .

I was up in three minutes and singing and dancing my butt off because I was, I *am* so much better than Courtney Schaeffer; and if she could do it, then I could do a whole lot better. No contest.

The strange thing was, the really strange thing was, at home that evening, tired but still buzzing, elated at having got all my decisions out of the way, I actually got my maths books out and had a look at – you know what I had a look at. The really strange thing was, I immediately understood, looking at my mum's drawings of sine and cosine waves, how the differential coefficient of sine x is cosine x. There it was, the rates of change of the curves plotting each other as they went. I sat there looking at it, seeing it, wondering how I'd managed to miss it for so long.

My dad was all over the place, excited by the promise of vast sums of money even more than I was excited by the fame. But my mum was subdued under the table-mountain of school exercise books she had to mark.

I went to her with my own books, laying them out by her side. She blinked seriously at me. 'Look,' I said, pointing to her wave drawings, 'the rate of change of the sine wave at zero is at its maximum, and at its maximum its rate of change is zero. If I only use those two co-ordinates alone, I can plot a cosine wave.'

She looked at me a long, long time. A long, long, long, long time. 'How did the recording go today?' she said.

'Fine,' I said. 'It's finished. I'm back at school tomorrow. I understand it, Mum, the differential of a trigonometrical function.'

'I know you do,' she said, going back to her marking, her red teacher's pen ticking and annotating each page.

My dad came to me, still coated in spaghetti-Lego, his hair an amalgam of styles and gel and mayonnaise: 'Your mum thinks you're wasting yourself,' he said, gripping my shoulder. 'I think it's great,' he whispered. I could smell baby food and fortified wine on his breath.

Even my maths wouldn't let me off completely. Looking at it and understanding suddenly was no help, not now I'd made up my mind. I needed the maths to remain incomprehensible, not to nod at me with a mock-friendly smile on its face like another Kirsten McCloud.

She, nodding to me mock-friendlily, squeezed a pinched

smile at me across the corridor. Kirsty had told no one about my big break with Solar Records. She pinched a poisonous smile in my direction before hurrying away without a word. Neither she nor Beccs asked me about what was happening at Solar.

I had a note from my father excusing me for the past few days, which said nothing about what I had been doing. At school, it was as if nothing had happened.

'Are we rehearsing this weekend?' I asked Beccs, when I saw her later in the day. I had to wait around for a long while before I could get her away from Kirsten for a few minutes.

She shook her head. 'Kirsty said she won't, so Geoff's not doing it.'

'What about you?' I asked.

She shrugged. 'Can't see the point,' she said. 'It won't work without Kirsty.'

'Why not?' I said.

Beccs seemed to step back, moving away from me physically. 'Why not? You seem to think all it needs is you, don't you? If anybody else leaves, it doesn't matter, as long as you're still there.'

'No! I don't think that at all.'

'No? Well you agree with me that there's no point in a Car Crime rehearsal without Kirsty and Geoff then, don't you.'

'Beccs,' I said, 'I didn't mean –'

'Becky,' she said. 'Remember? My name's Rebecca. That's Becky, to my friends.'

'All right. Becky. I didn't mean it didn't matter if they weren't there. I just meant – I just meant we could maybe rehearse anyway, you know, and see what we could do without –'

'Without her? You'd like that, wouldn't you?'

'No. But she'd like it without me there, wouldn't she?'

'No, as it happens. She's not the one trying to get you out, is she? She doesn't want to rehearse at all if you're off doing all your – your other stuff.'

'Oh, so that's it, is it?'

'No, it isn't, as it happens. This is it, if you really want to know. I'm fed up with having to put up with you having a go at my cousin – at my family and friends all the time. You've never liked her, have you? Have you!'

I was staring, astonished.

'No, you never have. But she's my friend. My *best* friend, if you must know. So I don't want to hear you going on about her, and I don't want to rehearse in your little second-fiddle dance-band without her there. Get it?'

Solar didn't call on me to do anything, so I didn't do anything. One weekend, two, three, I didn't do anything. I avoided Beccs and Kirsty, because they avoided me. Nothing happened. For ages, nothing looked like happening. My best friend said I wasn't her best friend any more. I had to go back to studying, to proving that:

If,   f (ax to the power of n)

Then $\dfrac{dy}{dx}$ = nax to the power of n − 1.

Yes, see if you can prove it. Especially when your mind is flitting every other half second onto what might, or not, be happening elsewhere. What were they doing? Nobody contacted me. I slaved over my differential equations, trying to think, trying not to think. My sisters started up a competition to see which one of them could get furthest down the loo. My dad spent his entire days walking like a zombie in the park or else building barricades to control access to different parts of the house. We all had to negotiate the barbed wire fences to go up to the bedrooms.

My mum didn't seem to be the teacher she once was. She wasn't enjoying what she was doing as she had before the twins. 'It's all right for you,' she blazed at my dad one evening during one of their rows, 'at least you get to spend some time with your family. At least you're not up to your neck correcting bad maths every day and every night!'

I ducked, up to my neck every day and every night as I was, trying to correct bad maths. It was all I could do to stop myself from being lonely. I couldn't stop myself; I was lonely. Ben had disappeared from school. Beccs wasn't playing football. Kirsty was posting pinched smiles to me from all over the place. Geoff was whispering from place to place, pale as a ghost.

My life was in limbo, but nothing looked like happening.

✱ Seventeen

Then it happened.

'You ready?' Ray Ray's voice came at me, full of Solar energy down the telephone line. 'You ready, or what? It's all lined up. Radio. Get this. Air play. One. In the Capital. All the biggies. I tell you, when I'm good, I'm good. You ready?'

'Yes,' I said, rather too tentatively.

'You better be. Because that's not all. Listen. Starlight. Charity. You listening? Three weeks' time. That's all. You.'

'What do you mean?'

'Single slot. Way down. But, listen. Starlight Charity Show-case. Benefit Cancer, once a year only. In three weeks. TV!'

'What?'

'You better believe it. Next week, week after, rehearsals, you. You gonna be ready, Amy Peppercorn. When Ray Ray make it happen, it happen.'

It happen. Ray Ray make it. Radio play. All the biggies.

School, three days later, it hit home. Wham! Bam! There was a commotion in the playground. First of all I thought it was trouble. Maybe it was, in a way. It was me. By the end of that same week, this little crowded commotion by the entr-ance gate waiting for me. Waiting for Amy Peppercorn.

'It's you, isn't it! It is you!'

'You were on the radio. Your name, and everything. She heard you!'

'How did you do it?'

'Are you going to make a video?'

'We've already made the video,' I said. I was smiling. The little crowd was following me into school.

'Great song,' one of the boys said.

'What's it called?'

'*The Word On The Street*,' I said, trying to remember that this was just my school, the place I'd been attending for years as an ordinary schoolgirl.

The ordinary schoolgirls and boys were treating me as if I was extraordinary. Which makes you feel extraordinary. Which actually makes you extraordinary. I was not like them any longer. Their ordinary excitement couldn't contain my extraordinary achievement. I was special. There aren't many girls of my age up to doing what I was doing.

That's how it goes, you see; one moment you're down, as way down as I'd been feeling, the next, you're up and flying. The lows dip as far as they do to give you a gauge against which to measure the highs. But still the highs are immeasurable, breathtaking, simply, truly wonderful.

'I knew it was you!' someone was calling.

'There aren't two Amy Peppercorns,' someone else said.

No, I thought, there are not two Amy Peppercorns. Something maybe in that name, something in being me, little me, that something had singled me out for this. I could feel the uniqueness immediately.

There I was, still at school, doing my ordinary stuff, living my day to day life; but in reality, yes, in reality, I was a real life pop singer with my first single starting to be played on the national radio channels.

'I'm on TV in a few weeks,' I boasted. Yes, I boasted. That's what success is for, isn't it, to boast about? I'd done something everyone else there would have loved to do. I'd become something, this soon in life.

'She's going on TV!' I heard the excited ripple whisper through the little crowd. Everyone would know about me now. I was going to be famous; there was no stopping it. Me, famous. Amy Peppercorn: how I had hated that name. How I now loved it. There were never two Amy Peppercorns. Just me! Just me!

Just me!

Not Kirsten, with her long, long legs and long hair. Just Amy Peppercorn, cutting a single, making a video, getting radio play. Going on TV in a few weeks. Amy Peppercorn, walking into the classroom for a double maths lesson as if I could concentrate on trig ratios and complex integrations. I had a little quirk of mad excitement in my stomach that kept tightening and making me want to laugh or scream. I couldn't sit still. The words of my song were flying through my head. I wanted to get up and sing it, right there and then, so everyone would be fully sure that it was me. Just me. Nobody but me!

Amy Peppercorn.

I kept saying my name. Soon everyone would be familiar with it. I'll be seen, on the screen. I! Me!

I couldn't work out why I hadn't been this excited all the way through. Then, when the bell rang and we all filed out of the classroom again, I knew why, only too well. The little crowd waiting outside with their excited questions and their jealous looks let me know why. I hadn't yet experienced this. This was what made it. Everything else came second to this, the feeling you get when everyone round you wants to know about you, wants to do what you're doing, wants to be you. That's what it was; the fact that they all wanted to be the thing I was, the very thing they'd all taken so much trouble to put down in the past. Now they all wanted to be under a metre and a half tall with mad short hair and a silly name like mine.

144

To think, I could so easily have not been me. The excitement of being exactly as I am, which is the very thing that hit singles and videos are made of. Little Amy Peppercorn is what I am, exactly as I would appear on the Starlight Charity Showcase, exactly reproduced on the televisions in all the homes in the whole of the country.

That quirk of excitement leapt and laughed with me as one of the boys wanted to be the first to get my autograph. It smiled tightly with me as Kirsten squeezed by in the corridor ignored by all the boys straining to get a closer look at me.

I didn't see Beccs all day. I didn't really want to. The day belonged to me. The need to justify myself just didn't arise. It might have been even better with Beccs, or Ben, with me, but I had no need to feel guilty about anything. The crowds all round, the admiring and the jealous looks I was getting were justification enough for me at the moment, thank you very much.

That evening, I called Beccs, just to let her know what was happening. She wasn't in. I tried. Her mum told me she was out with Kirsten.

'Who shall I say's calling?' Rebecca's mother was asking.

'It's Amy,' I said.

I put down the phone. Becca's mother didn't need to ask who was calling. She recognised my voice; she always had in the past. It wasn't that long since I'd called, was it? I couldn't remember.

I tried Ben's mobile; still the voice messaging system, still no answer. As soon as I put down the receiver again, it rang.

'Hello?'

'It's me.' It was Beccs. 'I just got in.'

145

'Where'd you go, anywhere nice?'

A pause. She had to think about it. 'Kirsty's. She's come back here with me now.'

'Oh,' I said. 'I was wondering if you – if you and Kirsty were going shopping at all tomorrow?'

There was another pause. 'Yes,' she said. 'We'll be there. We'll see you there, shall we?'

The one thing I would have liked, or loved, would have been to have Beccs on my side through all of this. She could have shared success with me. Why not? She'd been my best friend for years. For years I'd thought I was her best friend.

Now her mum was cagey in asking me who I was when I called and I was reduced in the friendship league to a see-you-there someone, an ex-Premiership player relegated to some-where much lower than the bottom of the Nationwide. Like in the mall in the shopping centre, when I had to hide and wait for Beccs and Kirsty to turn up late in their little skirts and tight tops.

'Hi,' Beccs said.

'Hi,' I said, trying not to look surprised; she'd been getting thinner for quite some time, but only now, in her surpris-ingly roomy short skirt, could I see just how much weight she'd lost.

'Hi,' Kirsty said, swaying like a sapling in the breeze.

'Oh, hi,' I said, looking quickly back at Beccs. 'Beccs,' I said, 'you're looking good.'

'Becky,' she said.

'Doesn't she look much better,' Kirsten started saying to me, without bothering to look at me. 'She feels much better too, don't you, Becky?'

Becky was swaying like a stunted Kirsten-tree, her looser skirt flipping across her thighs.

'Are you looking for anything in particular?' I asked, looking round at the shops.

'Oh,' Kirsten dashed in, saying, 'you know what we're like. We just keep looking and looking till we find something to suit our taste. You never really know what you like till you've tried it on.'

We started to walk through the mall, browsing in the shop fronts. Instinctively, we all walked into Shop-at-the-Top, the big department store, and stood without speaking on the downward-going escalator. As the stairs moved us into the basement Women's department, all we could hear was the music they played on the in-house radio station. All we could hear was a voice singing. It was my voice.

We looked over at the bank of video screens that combined to make one huge image. And there I was, singing and dancing my little butt off, leading my vee-formation dancers through our Solar routine. There I was, my in-your-face image magnified over the split screens like some kind of big girl-power pop star in the faces of the Shop-at-the-Top shoppers and my friends and me.

We stopped dead. My voice filled the store, just as if I was live and levelling my sound volume to fit the available shopping space. I looked quickly towards Beccs and Kirsten where they stood with their mouths open.

'Did you know that was going to happen?' Kirsten turned to me and said.

I stammered. 'No. No! How could I?'

I was as surprised as anyone. I was, in fact, shocked. To come across yourself unexpectedly like that was, in fact, shocking. It was like seeing yourself from the side for the first time, or hearing your recorded speaking voice, seeing and listening to yourself as others see and hear you, not as you appear face-on in the mirror or speaking safely inside

147

your own head. I had a copy of the vid, of course; but watching it with my surprisingly silent mum and dad and sisters did nothing to prepare me for this shock.

'She knew this was going to happen,' Kirsten turned to her cousin Becky and said. 'I bet she rigged this to happen as soon as we walked in the shop.'

'I didn't,' I said to Beccs. 'How could I?'

But Beccs was Kirsten's first cousin Becky, staring up at the multiplexed image of the dancers in their similar tight tops and girl-club training trousers.

'I've only come to do some shopping,' I said to Beccs, 'like you.'

She looked at me.

Kirsten had turned, was starting to walk away. 'I don't want to let her do this to me,' she was saying.

'I didn't do anything,' I said to Beccs.

She looked from me back to the screen. 'You've copied Courtney Schaeffer,' she said. She looked back at me again. 'You of all people! How many times have you told me how much you hated Courtney Schaeffer?'

Eighteen

We had four days to rehearse for the show. My mum was saying nothing about it, about me taking Monday to Thursday away from school again to be ready for Saturday night. My dad was all over the place, shouting down the telephone to his parents, to his brother and sister, to his friends, to the operator, to directory enquiries, to anybody that would listen. He was telling the world to watch the Starlight Charity Showcase on TV on Saturday evening. He was telling them, above the everyday and everynight cries of his younger daughters, that his eldest would be on the show. Yes, actually performing a song, a soon-to-be-on-its-way-up-the-charts pop song, on the Starlight Charity Showcase in aid of Cancer Research. He wanted to call the local papers, to tell them; but my mother stopped him, telling him that wouldn't be necessary.

She was watching him silently over her pile of exercise books. She'd been glancing up at him as he juggled Jo and George, all three of them screaming in the general direction of the telephone receiver. 'Yes! She's – yes! Amy! A record. It's called – what's it called again? – Yes. On Saturday!'

As soon as he put the twins down, they were climbing up his trouser legs. He was holding up his belt with one hand, holding the telephone with the other.

I'd been rehearsing dance routines for hours on end. For the video, all you need is a few seconds at a time. They edit out the flops and the falls later. All you have to do is pretend to sing. You sing, but it doesn't really matter if it goes wrong. But for a live performance, the whole thing has to come together from the beginning to the end. Every step and every word have to be in synch, or you're sunk.

Every muscle in my body was aching. All I could do was sit at the other end of the table from my mum's exercise books, pretending to eat the food my dad had thrown onto my plate.

'I know!' he cried, tugging at his trousers. He had a twin suspended on each leg, his wet knees sopping with saliva. 'I know! The local rag! Why haven't the locals been round for a story?'

As he reached for the telephone again, my mother said, 'Tony, calm down. That won't be necessary. They'll be here, after the show. Just, calm, down.'

'I am calm,' he said, marching round with Jo and Georgie perched on his feet. 'What makes you think I'm not calm? – I know! Your uncle in the States. We could send them a copy of the video. Let me call him. What's his number?'

'Tony, you are not calling America. Calm *down*.'

'I am calm. I told you. Oops, look out. There go my trousers. No, not my – Ow! Not the hairs on my – Ow! – legs. Jo! George! Ow! You little pests!'

'Tony!' my mum cried. 'I need to concentrate. Please.'

'Oh, do stop being such a schoolmistress for a few minutes, can't you? Celebrate!'

'What,' she said, 'you haven't gone and found yourself a job, have you?'

'Very funny,' he said.

It wasn't very funny. Neither of them was laughing, all of a sudden. I could see what was coming, but was too tired to duck out of the way. I could have done with a little peace and quiet. I could have done with a little more support from my friends and my family. Instead, I got silence from the one, this row from the other.

'Have you even been looking for a job?'

'How can I, with these two every day? How'm I supposed to look for a job with these two? Anyway, what's wrong with the way it is now?'

'The way it is now? I thought you hated being at home?'

'And I thought you loved being a teacher?'

'Well you thought wrong, didn't you?'

'So did you, because I'm doing all right. But you hate it whenever I'm doing all right, don't you!'

'No! That's not fair!'

'No, I know it's not fair. Nothing's fair. It doesn't matter what happens, you're never satisfied.'

'And you are, I suppose?'

'Yes, I am. All right? I am satisfied, all right? I'm doing fine. The twins are doing fine, aren't they? Aren't they?'

'Yes! All right? Yes!'

'Amy's doing great, isn't she? Isn't she?'

Yes, Amy was doing great; silence from non-existent friends, this from family, and a copy of the programme for the Starlight Charity Showcase, showing the order of appearance of all the performers, with me very near the bottom, and a certain Ms Courtney Schaeffer plumped right up the very top.

'Amy's doing great isn't she? She's going to show them all, aren't you, Amy? She's going to be the next Courtney Schaeffer, aren't you Amy?'

And the dance routines we had to follow had all been rehearsed by Courtney, so many times in the past.

'Aren't you, Amy? You're going to be the next Courtney Schaeffer, aren't you?'

151

And all the words I sing are Courtney's words reworked; because, as I found out this week, those two old song writers used to be Courtney's song writers before she got rich and famous enough to choose songs from wherever she liked the most.

'Is that what you are then?' my mum was asking. 'I'm Courtney Schaeffer's mother now, am I?' she was saying. 'And I thought I was Amy Peppercorn's mother. Is that what you are now then, Amy? I'm sorry, I didn't know.'

'Don't start getting at her,' my dad said, pointing at me, 'she hasn't done anything.'

'I know she hasn't.'

'Neither have I!' he shouted. 'All I've done is stay at home to look after the twins, like you said, so you could go back to work, like you said. But you don't like it, do you? You don't like it because I like it, do you? You don't like it because I'm actually good at it. That's it, isn't it?'

My mum was on her feet wailing, declaring that that wasn't it at all. 'Not at all!' she declared.

'What is it then?' my dad was demanding to know.

I sat at the dining table with my family shouting and screaming round me, but at the same time I was out there being a cheaper, certainly smaller copy of Courtney; recognised as being a lesser her by my family and friends and foes, and all the other wannabe look-alikes practising Courtney steps and pouts and poses in front of their bedroom mirrors every night, week after week. In here, in the din of our dining room, my parents and guardians roared at each other because neither of them were or seemed to know what they wanted to be, while I sat trying not to be turned into something out there I never liked nor cared to emulate. My little sisters wailed as the world tried to alter us all to fit. Nobody, it seemed, could be what they wanted to be.

I looked at little Jo and Georgie as they cried, their almost identical tongues quivering in their open mouths, wailing at the way of the world. My one Courtney-copy hit would certainly come and go in no time and leave me wailing for what I would have been, should have been without it. I should have been in a band with Ben Lyons and my friends. We should have been having fun, making some music while we're young, music from ourselves and for ourselves.

My songwriters were grim, grey hit-meisters from a pre-Courtney era, my record company a hit-making monster turning the graves of the real music-makers, looking under their headstones for scraps of ideas to rework and recycle over and over. I was just the latest in the eternal line of mouth-pieces, little one-hit-wonders with nothing to them other than a pre-emptive school-leaving and a serial string of broken relationships.

The one thing – the two things I wanted most, were to talk to and to be friends with Beccs, and to see and be with Ben. He'd kissed me once, in this house, in the hall by the front door, but I'd missed it, as I seemed to have missed most things. Solar Records were in the business of making money. So was I. It was different and separate to my own interests and friendships.

I had one day, Friday, at school, before the Charity Performance evening on Saturday; one day to see everybody, to let them know that I am not Courtney. I am me: Amy Peppercorn. That's who I am. I wanted them all to see that. I was way down the appearance list on Charity Performance night; Courtney was way at the top. There was a difference. A very big difference.

But on Friday morning, I had to practically fight my way into the school building. We were all made late. The place was a pandemonium, with jammed corridors and empty class-rooms. The teachers were trying to organise the chaos back into normality; they were failing. Everyone, it seemed, was being whipped up into a frenzy of wanting to be close to me, to speak to me and touch me on the arm. I felt so special, so very gifted. Touching me, they seemed to want to take a little bit of my specialness away with them, all the little girls and boys.

Our Headmaster, Mr Headingly, had to wade through the milling crowd to get to me. He led me into the school hall, onto the stage. All the other teachers were instructed to gather all the classes in the hall for what the Head called an 'impromptu assembly'. We had to wait there, the Headmaster and me, while everyone in the whole school filed in and was seated, all looking towards where we stood on the stage together, watching the assembly. All the school faces were turned to the front, looking up at me as I fidgeted next to the Head, as he directed, pointing at and nodding to the teachers. I started to worry that he was going to ask me to sing something right there and then, in front of everyone, with no music and without my confidence. I was thinking that I might tug on his sleeve to get him to listen to me telling him I couldn't do it, when he started to clap his hands slowly, raising his hands in the air for silence.

'I'm sure –' his great strong voice blared out beside me, almost making me jump. 'Can we have complete silence, please? – I said, SILENCE! Yes. – I'm sure you've all heard that we've got a new celebrity here amongst us,' he bellowed, glancing at me.

I felt as if I'd done something wrong by him; that my punishment was about to be announced. I looked out at Mrs

McKintyre, my Biology tutor; she looked as if she thought so too.

'And I know,' the Head went on, 'how interested we all are to find out what Amy has done. It is only natural to be curious – to be fascinated by this – by this sort of thing. The one thing, I'm sure, that we all would like to do, is to congratulate Amy, Amy, we believe you are to appear on the Starlight Charity Showcase tomorrow?'

I nodded, finding myself blushing as he said it.

'Congratulations,' he said to me. Turning back to the assembled school, he said: 'The Starlight Showcase this year is sponsoring Cancer Research. A very worthy cause. Isn't that so, Amy?'

I nodded again, blushing more furiously.

The Head turned back to the assembly again. 'I think that deserves a round of applause, don't you?'

They did, evidently, as a cheer went up and the applause broke out as if it had been waiting impatiently in the wings. As the school clapped for me, I caught sight of two faces peering cheerlessly at the back of the hall. There were quite a few not cheering or clapping or smiling, but Kirsten's and Becky's faces stood out for the distaste, for the disgust they were showing.

Mr Headingly had his hands in the air again, trying to end the applause as I noticed Geoffrey Fryer, also at the back of the hall, but across the other side. The clapping was abating, but Geoffrey was receiving a couple of claps, quite hard, one on each ear, from the seats immediately behind him. Peter Stevens and Michael Bradshaw grinned and slapped Geoff's head from side to side in a grotesque parody of the applause I was receiving without the other Car Crime members.

'However,' Mr Headingly was blasting by my side, 'however, this *is* a school. We are all here for a specific purpose. I sincerely hope I need not remind you of what that purpose is.'

He left a pause there, in case anybody cared to laugh at his schoolmaster's joke; nobody did. I was looking at Geoffrey as he cowered, red eared and disturbed, but not laughing, at the back of the hall just in front of the spiteful and vengeful New Grunge Machine.

'So,' Mr Headingly went on, 'I think we all need to turn our concentration towards the purpose of this establishment. We have already lost, what, twenty minutes' school time; we cannot, any of us, including Amy, afford to lose any more. So, while we all wish Amy every success and look forward to seeing her on TV tomorrow, today is another valuable school day. Let's not waste it. I want you all, starting with Year Seven, to file out, in good order, and make your way to your form rooms. If you please!'

Poor Geoffrey Fryer received another slap, if you please! He was not pleased; neither was I. Ben, as far as I could see, was not there. Geoff wouldn't have been slapped like that if he had been, I was sure.

'Amy!' the Headmaster called to me as I went to make off after Beccs and Kirsty.

'Where are you going in such a hurry?'

'I have to – my lesson. My maths. I have to go.'

'Oh,' he said. 'Perhaps I could have a word later? I'd like to, you know – my daughter wanted me to get your autograph. You don't have any signed photos, do you?'

I ran off after Beccs and Kirsty as they busied up the corridor together. They were always together now, I knew, especially as they turned towards me as I called them, and I could see again just how much weight Beccs had lost – and how the Becky-highlights in her longer hair badly emulated her first cousin's sleek and shining, somehow hostile hair.

'Hey!' I called.

They turned. 'It's Courtney,' Kirsten said, loud enough to ensure that I heard it. Rebecca didn't bother to hide her amusement.

'Haven't you two seen what's been happening to Geoff?' I said, running up to them.

Kirsty looked up to the ceiling. Becky just looked at me, her face surprisingly thin and surprisingly unsuited to it.

'Look,' I said, 'I've only been back a few minutes and I've seen what's going on. You must have seen something, you two?'

A couple of other girls had stopped, were trying to listen to what was going on between us.

'Oh,' Kirsten said to the girls, 'she's only been back a few minutes and she's seen what's going on. She sees everything, doesn't she, even though she's so very little?'

A few boys were also standing round now, instead of going off to their delayed first lesson, listening with undisguised amusement.

'Beccs,' I said.

'Becky,' she said, immediately.

I stopped. I hadn't meant to call her Beccs, because she looked so much like a Becky-girl; the force of old fond habit formed the word before I could amend it. I stopped.

'She doesn't want to be called that any more,' Kirsten said, 'do you Becky?'

Rebecca was looking at me, as I was at her. 'Whatever,' I said. 'I don't think I care. It's Geoff I care about, at the moment.'

'Superstar,' Kirsten sneered.

The corridor was becoming crowded. We were being pushed together. 'Amy Peppercorn!' someone was shouting from the back of the crowd.

'Courtney Schaeffer,' Kirsten was saying.

The growing crowd crowded in on us, suddenly shoving me towards Kirsten and Rebecca. I had to put my hand out to prevent myself stumbling. Kirsten swiped it away.

'Come on, Becky,' she said, turning, shoving her way through the crowd. 'I've had enough of this.'

'Geoff needs our help,' I said to Rebecca.

Kirsten turned. 'Oh, yeah? Like we helped him before? Like the way you manipulated everybody, that kind of help?'

'Don't let her do this,' I said to Rebecca.

'Like your kind of help that only helps yourself,' Kirsten was railing at me now, letting out all her long-held frustrations. 'Like that kind of help, is that what you mean?'

'They're getting at Geoff,' I said to Rebecca. 'Beccs –'

'Don't call me that again,' she said.

I stopped. She was supposed to be my friend. My friend was called Beccs.

'What do you want?' Kirsten said, bending right down to speak into my face.

A few out of the corridor crowd had started singing my song. Rebecca glanced round. 'You can help him,' I said to her.

'I'm not helping him,' Kirsten said. 'What's the matter with him? Let him stand up for himself. I've had him hanging round me for too long. Leave me out of it. Come on, Becky.'

Rebecca glanced at her.

'Come and help him, Becca,' I said.

'No,' Kirsten said, 'come with me, Becky. Come on.'

'Don't just leave him,' I said. 'Rebecca, you wouldn't do that. I know you wouldn't.'

'Come on,' Kirsten said, pulling her against the crush of the crowd.

'Beccs,' I said, trying to pull her back.

A great roaring voice sounded over the crowd in the choked corridor. 'What's going on here?'

Beccs was looking at me.

'Amy Peppercorn!' the great voice of Mr Headingly the Headmaster boomed out, drowning the general racket and dispersing the crush of the fans I never knew I had. 'I knew you were at the centre of this,' he boomed at me, as the crowd scattered and Kirsten led Rebecca away with her.

Beccs was glancing back at me as Mr Headingly told me he was going to escort me to my maths class to prevent any further disruption.

'Can you just sign this for me?' he was saying, as Beccs, led by Kirsten in one direction, glanced back at me; and I, led by the nose by Head Headingly, glanced back from the other direction I was being forced into taking.

✱✱✱ Nineteen

Twenty or thirty times I must have called him, maybe more: 'Ben! As soon as you get this message, call me back!' 'Ben! Where are you? Call me!' 'Ben! You'd better call me!'

I called his home number. His mother told me he was at school. 'He'll be home later though,' she said, 'I suppose.'

'What time will he be home?' I asked.

'Now then,' his mother mused. 'Now that's a fair question. I couldn't be saying now exactly, not *exactly* what time we'll be expecting to see him. But we'll see him. No doubt about it.'

I left my name and mobile phone number, then went back to calling his mobile, leaving message after message. 'Ben! Turn on your phone! You are such a useless – Ben! Call me back! I know you've got my number!'

I'd seen Geoff by that time, just him and me in another classroom. This time, there were faces pressed hard against the glass panel of the door, peering round the corner to try to see what was going on. I had the door jammed closed with a chair.

'We know what you're do-ing!' they were chanting outside.

'I'm al-al-all r-right,' Geoff was saying, his eyes avoiding my own.

I was trying to get him to look at me, to see if I could see into him. 'Geoff,' I said, 'I saw them hitting you.'

He was shaking his head. 'I'm al-all r-right,' he was repeating, again and again. 'You d-don't need t-t-t-to w-worry about me.'

'Geoff,' I said, 'I am worried about you.'

'D-d-don't then,' he said. 'I'm al-al-all r-r-r –'

'No, Geoff,' I said, 'you're not all right.'

He was not all right, evidently. He was far from all right. I needed to help him, to get help for him. I needed to speak to Ben.

Geoffrey wouldn't look at me. He kept glancing at the jammed door as if he wanted to run out and away. I felt that he did: to run out of the school and run away from everything and everybody determined to make his life a living misery. There he was, telling me he was all right, when every movement he made, every expression on his face showed how very un-alright he really was.

'Geoff,' I said again, as a wild crash shuddered through the chair jammed against the door handle. Geoffrey's body movement and facial expressions showed what he was being put through. He couldn't look at me.

'Grunge Machine isn't finished with you, Fryer,' someone, probably Peter Stevens, growled from the corridor.

'You can't hide,' another voice, possibly Michael Bradshaw's, hissed through the rattling gaps of the jammed door. 'Grunge always knows where you are.'

'They can't do this to you,' I turned and said.

His face was white. His whole long body looked as if it wanted to fold down smaller than me, tucking itself away somewhere safe they would *not* know, where he *could* hide, until the Grunge *were* finally finished with him.

The door crashed and crashed again as I watched Geoff's white face wince and wince again. I reached out, intending to touch his arm, to grip him for a moment, trying to let him

161

know he was not alone in this. But Geoffrey saw my hand coming and dodged away from it to the door that had fallen to rest on its silent hinges.

He looked out through the glass window in the door. 'They've g-gone. I've g-g-got to g-g –'

'Geoff,' I said, halting his hand on the door handle.

'D-don't d-do anything,' he said, turning towards me, almost in tears.

'I can help,' I said. 'You need some help.'

'What,' he said, 'l-l-l-like the help you g-got for me be-before? Help l-like that?'

'Geoff, I –'

'The only p-person you – you – you ever help, A-Amy, is y-you.' He took a deep breath, looking at me now. 'The only person you ever help,' he said, deliberately, word-perfectly quoting the poison Kirsten had been pouring into his ear, 'is you.'

'That's not true,' I said.

Geoff looked away from me.

'That's not true,' I said, softly, to myself: to myself, because Geoff had gone. The crowd outside the door had gone. 'It just isn't true,' I said to myself, reaching into my bag for my mobile phone.

'Ben! You better call me! I have to talk to you! Ben! Call me!'

'Ben! Call me!'

'Ben!'

His mother, in her thick brogue, told me Ben was already with me, here, at school. I looked around the empty class-room, outside into the deserted corridor, down towards the entrance to, or exit from, the building. Ben was never there. His mother seemed to think he was. I asked her to get him to call me. She said she didn't know when she was expecting to see him; just like me, as I stalked through the playground angry and too early out of school, heading for home still yelling into my mobile: 'Ben! I have to see you. Be at the big video store in the town tonight at seven. Be there!'

Several times, ten, eleven, twelve times I buzzed Ben's voicemail, leaving another after another insistent message. 'Be there at seven tonight. You better be there!'

'What time is it?' my dad turned and said as I came in too early. 'What are you doing? What's happened?' He was reading the paper at the kitchen table. Georgie and Jo were doing the washing-up. 'Are you okay?' he said.

'I'm fine,' I said, wading ankle deep in the bubbles from the bowl of soapsuds and plastic bowls my sisters were tossing into the air and not catching. The kitchen was coated in a soapy film of burst bubbles. 'Shouldn't you be – Dad, do you think this is a good idea?' I said, indicating the rainbow floor and kitchen cabinets and chairs.

He peered at the girls from the side of his newspaper. 'What? Oh, don't worry about that. I do it every day now. It's baby bath bubbles, not washing up liquid. When they've soaked everything, I hose it all down. Instant clean kids and kitchen in one go. Good, eh?'

I looked at the mess. 'If you say so, Dad.'

'I say so,' he said. 'I also say, I'm getting very good at this lark. Dinner's prepared and in the oven, no worries. Why are you home so early?'

'I – need to be ready for tomorrow.'

'Yes, you do. It's so exciting, isn't it? Are you excited? I am. So's your mum, in her own way. Early night for you then, is it?'

'Maybe. I've got to go out.'

'Where?'

'To see a friend. I'll not be late.'

'No, don't be. What shall I tell your mother?'

'Tell her – tell her she's Amy Peppercorn's mother, not Courtney Schaeffer's.'

He blinked at me. 'She already knows,' he said.

'Does she?' I said. 'Do you?'

Seven o'clock came and went. I waited. I waited and I waited. I was too early, wanting to be sure to be out by the time my mother got home. She might be early, so I was out very early.

I waited. A boy on the street opposite the video shop said to me: 'You're that girl, aren't you.' It wasn't a question. You're that girl. 'There's that girl,' he went and told his little mate.

That girl walked away from them. I was too early. I was too famous locally, being that girl the kids on the street noticed, recognised from my face in the local paper, from the copies of my CD the record shop up the way were selling. They were selling hundreds of them, by all accounts. 'You're going on that Courtney Schaeffer show tomorrow, aren't you,' one told me, as I walked away again.

Seven o'clock came and went. I waited until my patience ran out, stabbing the buttons of my mobile with a hard held finger.

'Okay, okay,' Ben's voice came immediately onto the line. 'I'm on my way.'

'There you are!' I shouted into my phone. 'Why didn't you call me?'

'I'm on my way,' he said, just before the line went dead. I watched the face of my mobile changing back to its standby mode as a souped and serious little white rally sports car pulled up in front of the video store and in front of me. There was nobody in the passenger seat. Bending, I looked into the car to see Ben Lyons sitting in the driver's seat with his far arm hooked out of the open window.

The passenger window through which I was looking, wound down automatically. 'Get in,' Ben said, with just the briefest of glances at me.

'What you doing?' I cried into the window. 'What you think you're –'

'Get in!' Ben shouted.

'I'm not getting in there, with you. What are you – is this car stolen? Of course it's stolen! What are you *on*? You must be –'

'Are you just going to stand there insulting me?' he said, turning to look at me.

'Listen,' I said, 'I needed to talk to you. Geoff's in trouble at school. He needs your help. But you're just a –'

'Are you getting in,' he said, 'or what?'

I slapped the roof of the car. 'What *is* the matter with you?'

'I'm going,' he said. 'Are you getting in, or not?'

I looked up and down the road.

'Bye, Amy,' Ben said.

'No!' I said. 'Wait. Hold on.' I opened the car door. 'I don't want to go to any stupid car park for any stupid races or anything, all right?'

He nodded.

'You just drive round the block, slowly, right?'

Ben just looked forward through the windscreen at the road.

'Right?' I shouted at him.

'All right,' he said. 'All right. Come on, get in. I'll take it easy. Come on.'

I climbed into the passenger seat. The car was pure boy-racer, built black speedster interior, smelling of soft new vinyl and travel sickness. Ben drove the thing as if he drove himself about every day; which, I had the feeling, perhaps he did.

'Why are you doing this?' I said.

He didn't say anything. He might have shrugged, I don't know; I wasn't looking. It felt as if he shrugged.

'You must be crazy,' I told him.

'Yeah,' he said, 'I must be.'

The light was going. Street lamps were blinking on here and there.

'You *are* crazy,' I said. 'Why haven't you been to school?'

His no-answer shrugged at me again.

'Ben,' I cried, turning to him, 'why are you doing this? You told me it wasn't right for you. You said –'

'Did I say that? I didn't know what I was talking about. This is the next thing.'

'Oh, yes? And what's the thing after that, eh? And the thing after that?'

He did shrug this time, physically, as I looked at him. 'More speed, isn't it,' he said. 'Car Crime. Really. You wouldn't understand.'

'No,' I said, 'I wouldn't. No one could understand, because there's no sense in it. It's stupid. Where's it going to get you?'

'I don't care where it gets me!'

'Oh! Come on! You're just being –'

'I'm just being me, all right? This is what I do, what I am. All right? It's got nothing to do with you, or anyone. If you like, I'll let you out, right now.'

'Yeah, all right then. No, you take me back to the video shop. You take me back and just listen to me. Geoff needs your help. He's getting all kinds of grief from Stevens and Bradshaw. He can't handle it.'

'What do you want *me* to do?'

'Well what do you think you *can* do? You can help him, you know you can.'

'Why can't you?'

'Because I can't any more. It's –'

'Too busy, I suppose, are you? Too busy being a Courtney Schaeffer, eh?'

I looked out of the window, breathing heavily. The evening was coming on. We were flitting by the flickering streetlamps quite fast now, moving up a gear in anger, the both of us.

'Look,' I said, 'what would you have done, if you were me?'

'I'm not you, am I. I'm me. You do what you do, I'll do what I do.'

'Ben, you're such an idiot. *Such* an idiot – do you know that?'

'And you're not, I suppose. I wouldn't have done what you're doing, that's for sure. I wouldn't have done that. How long do you think it's going to last, eh?'

'Not long,' I said, looking back at the angrily flitting streetlamps.

'What do you think you're going to get out of it? All the little kids following you round, are they? Bet that feels good.'

'It does, all right? Yes, it does. You should try it. But you can't can you, because they didn't want you. They didn't want the others. They didn't want Kirsten. They didn't want Car Crime or any of your ideas. They wanted me. Right?'

'Yeah, right. For the minute.'

'Yeah, the minute. It'll do for me. I'm on TV tomorrow in the –'

'Oh, well done.'

'Yes, I think so. I *do* think so. Hardly anybody else could have done it. I've done it.'

'Yeah, well done. You'll be doing all right at school as well, will you?'

'I'm not doing all right at school. I'm just not. It doesn't matter. This is something else. I can do something else.'

'So can I!' Ben said, stating his full-stop fact very loudly. 'I can do something else as well. My thing won't last long, but neither will yours. And what's the next thing for you then, Amy? And the thing after that, and the thing after that?'

'Slow down!' I shouted, as much at what he was saying, at what he was throwing at me, as at his faster and faster driving. 'Slow down I said! What's the matter with you?'

'What's the matter with *you*?' he shouted back, without slowing anything. 'You can criticise me, but I can't say anything back to you. Why is that Amy? Eh? Answer me!'

We were approaching a roundabout at insane miles an hour, with the lighted streetlamps flitting by the corners of my eyes as I tried to focus on the quickly approaching junction. 'Slow down! For God's sake! What are you trying to do? Ben!'

We were tearing round the roundabout. My shoulder was shoving hard against the door. I reached down to ensure my seatbelt was safely fastened. 'Ben! For God's sake! All right! I understand what you're doing!'

'No you don't!' he screamed, spinning the steering wheel, driving us forward too fast into the next then the next mile of road, unwinding too quickly to meet us.

'Ben!' I screamed. 'That's enough!'

'Look behind!' he shouted.

As I did, the siren of the blinking police car wildly on our tail started up its wail. The officer in the passenger seat gesticulated for us to pull over. 'Oh God!' I swore, swinging back round in my seat. 'Oh my God! Ben! Pull over.'

'I can't, can I. How can I pull over?'

'Ben, you're going to kill – Ben! For God's sake!' I was screaming as we took another mad roundabout heavy with sideways centrifugal force. I found myself leaning forward, holding on to the passenger half of the dashboard. 'Ben! You're going to get us killed!'

'Hold on and shut up! I know what I'm doing!'

The streetlamps were flitting by like another pulse at the sides of my head. We were driving even faster as we approached the next junction towards the town. I screamed as Ben pulled out straight onto the main road without slowing or looking. Cars were swerving to avoid us. Hooters were blaring, headlights blazing. I was screaming.

Ben was shouting me down: 'Shut the – Shut up! Shut up!'

'You're going to get us killed!' I wailed.

We were approaching the town centre, weaving in and out of all the other cars with the police car still sitting hard and fast on our tail. I couldn't look round now, but knew the police were there, so close our car's interior was lighting up, flashing with blue light. My ears were full of the siren's wail and my own screams and Ben's shouts to try and shut me up.

'You'll have to stop!' I screamed. 'You'll have to! There's nowhere to go. They're going to get us. You're going to spoil everything. There's nowhere to go!'

'There's always somewhere to go,' he shouted, as we sped up the road to the shopping centre, tearing and screeching round a sudden corner into a side street.

'Oh my God,' I said, watching the end of the dead-end street careering towards us. 'Oh my God!' with the police car inches from our back bumper.

We hurtled towards the end of the road. I screamed as we drove madly towards the metal posts that were cemented between the pavement and the road. I closed my eyes, clenching them and my teeth and everything else ready for the crash and crunch of this horrible little car and my own bones.

But Ben screamed. He wailed like a banshee in his aggressive joy and victory. I opened my eyes to find us hurtling through the small space between two buildings, nothing more than an alley really. I glanced behind to see the police car stalled on the other side, too wide to have made it through the metal pedestrian posts.

We flew out the other side into a service road, smashing round another small roundabout before accelerating at a scream's pace towards another main road. Ben was screaming with delight, his crazed head and arms thrashing, pounding the steering wheel and the vinyl of his door. 'Yes!' he was wailing. 'Yes! Yes! Yes!'

I couldn't breathe. The flying streetlamps were flashing at a malevolent frequency into the corners of my eyes. I was dizzy with fear and hyperventilating. My ears and head were full of Ben's crazed savage cry. 'Yes! Got them! You see that? Yes! See that? Did you see that? Yes! Yes!'

My breath was coming and going, coming and going. The lights outside were inside with me, were actually inside me. My head was hammering. My cheeks and eyes felt as if they were about to burst.

I opened my mouth to beg Ben to slow down. His scream came out of me. It went into me again. I opened my mouth to let it out. I opened my mouth to breathe. My wide-open eyes broke down the flashing lights with striped blocks of dark. There was a vinyl sickness somewhere near. There was an insurmountable tension, a pressure closing in from the bottom of the sea.

Ben's last scream disappeared from my side. The pressure of the dark sea closed in on me, shutting me down, shutting me down.

170

*** Twenty

Then, suddenly, I was at home. My mum and dad were worried about me. My mum was worried because I'd bruised myself so much in the car; my dad was worried that it was going to interfere with the Starlight Charity Showcase. They had me in bed before I could even begin to remember what had happened.

'We'd best leave you to get your sleep,' my dad softly said.

The house was quiet. It was dark outside, but I didn't know what time it was. My whole body ached. There was an enormous throbbing from my ankle where I must have hit it.

Ben must have brought me home in the car. I didn't know what my parents would have made of that, but I was too tired to worry. My after-epileptic-fit body ached for sleep.

But sleep brought fast cars careering down madly flickering streets. It brought car chases through the house where my silent sisters played, where my mother and father looked on in horror as we came crashing through. All the Car Crime members were yelling and spitting and hating each other for the crimes we were accusing each other of having committed.

I woke to my own bedroom at the end of a long car chase. My dreams were like films, but personally insulting. They tired me out.

There was a stage show. I dreamt of waiting in the wings while jugglers and fire-eaters and acrobats attacked each other, squirming and thrashing and striking out with blazing

171

juggling clubs. Then suddenly Courtney Schaeffer was centre-stage singing my song, running through my dance routine and I couldn't stop her or the audience from appreciating what she was doing far more than they would like me. I woke again, still sick with the feeling of nothing left to offer now that she had stolen my act, my thunder.

It was light outside. The feeling that Courtney Schaeffer was so much better, had so much more to offer than I did, was still powerfully with me. The feeling that both Ben and I were on an ultra-brief career to disappointment or disaster was there too, just as powerfully.

It must have been very early, I thought, because of the silence of a dawn that sounded like songbirds and not like screaming brats. But then I heard some movement just outside my bedroom door, lowered voices like those of my parents but softer, much, much quieter. The atmosphere, the unobtrusive whispers, sounded like a house in mourning. I touched my arms, pressing bruises to be sure of the pains of being still alive.

Yes, I was here. I'd obviously had a pretty bad seizure in that stolen car next to Ben. I could just about remember being dropped off by him at home. The concerned faces of my parents came to me vaguely as if from one of the night's restive dreams.

A surprisingly powerful lurch of hunger moved me as I looked at my bedside clock. It wasn't nearly as early as I'd thought. In fact, considering everything I was going to have to do today, it was quite late. I jumped out of bed. My ankle tried to stab me with a pain, which I chose to ignore.

The house seemed deserted. Nobody moved. There was no sound, other than a far-off radio or television set with the news on.

'Where are the twins?' I said, coming into the living room

where my parents, side by side on the settee, were watching the news. Their heads turned towards me together.

'There you are,' my dad said. 'We were worried about you. How are you feeling now?'

'Hungry,' I said. 'Why's the house so quiet?'

'Your father took the twins to his sister last night,' my mother explained, turning to look more closely at me. She looked worried. 'You gave us all a fright,' she said, shaking her head.

I tried to smile.

'Your father took the twins over to try to give you a decent rest.'

'Nightmare journey,' he started to say. 'Both screaming the windscreen out all the way. Had them strapped in their child-seats in the back. Should have had them gagged too; or strapped to the roof.'

'You're both watching the telly,' I said, 'on a Saturday morning,' as I started for the kitchen to get my breakfast.

'Special day, today,' my dad said.

'What were you doing,' my mother was calling to me, with the worry still in her voice, 'in that car, with him, last night?'

'Nothing,' I called to her.

'I didn't know he had a car,' my mother called, as I poured my milk over my cereal.

I took the bowl back into the living room with me. 'What?' I said.

'Special day,' my dad was saying. 'My little girl, on the telly, live. You all right now?'

'Did you forget your –' my mum started to say.

'No,' I interrupted, 'I took my tablets. It must be the stress. The excitement, I mean.'

'That boy had to bring you home,' my mum said.

'Nice little car, though,' my unworried dad said.

'Ben, that's his name, isn't it?' my mum said.

'Yes,' I said. 'Ben. He's – the car's his dad's, I think.'

'That's all right then,' my dad said.

'He's insured, and everything?' my mum was looking at me.

'How you feeling this morning, then?' my dad looked round at me and said, as I sat in front of the television.

'I'm feeling fine,' I said.

My mum still looked worried. She could see I was having trouble looking at her. 'You had a nasty fit,' she was saying. 'Are you sure you're all right? That's quite a bruise you've got on your ankle. I saw it there last night.'

'She's fine,' my dad was saying, watching the Saturday morning TV advertisements.

'That boy?' my mum was asking. 'Isn't he the same age as you?'

I was watching the screen.

'The same age as me?' my dad said, still watching the TV.

'Not you!' she snapped. 'Amy. What's someone your age doing driving round in fast little sports cars like that one, that's what I'd like to know?'

'He's older than me, Mum. He drives to school.'

My dad laughed. 'Imagine that. Drives to school. Whatever next, eh?'

My mum looked at me as if I was lying. 'Are you sure?'

I was lying. 'Of course I'm sure. Don't go on. He's safe.'

'He's safe,' my dad said, nodding towards the TV. 'Drives to school every day.'

My mother shook her head at him. 'Are you sure you're okay?' She said, looking seriously at me. 'I'm worried about you.'

'I know you are,' I said. 'You don't need to be.'

'Don't worry,' my dad said. 'She's fine, aren't you, Amy?'

I nodded, swallowing my breakfast cereal, looking at the screen. A motor ad came on, with some kind of saloon car smoking through a valley of volcanic eruption and fire.

'You nervous, are you?' my dad said, without looking at me. 'About tonight?'

I shivered. I could see a car dashing by at high speed, travelling at – at epileptic miles an hour, at a confusing frequency of passing streetlamps flickering on and off, spinning, dizzying. A thin sweat broke out on my face. I swallowed hard breakfast cereal in crackling lumps, wiping the cold milk and moisture from my top lip. 'Yes,' I said. Yes, I felt nervous, I suppose. If that means when your neural system is on edge and popping, like, say, just after a nasty epileptic seizure, then you could say I felt nervous. I felt speedy, restive, unrested, looking over the horizon at a migraine sprinkled and fizzing in the near future.

'Yes,' my dad said. 'You must be nervous. What a night, eh? Amy?'

'Yes,' I said.

'Jill?' he said. 'What a night, eh?'

'Yes,' she said, blinking, as I was, at the car-crazy television screen.

I glanced at Jill, at my mum. She, I was sure, felt as detached from everything as I did. She was left feeling as confused at her own lack of satisfaction at becoming a teacher again as I was at playing my part in appearing on tonight's show, singing one of Courtney Schaeffer's cast-offs and performing a dance Courtney could do much better in her, and in my own, sleep.

'What time's the car coming for you?' my dad was bouncing, trying to instil his lonely enthusiasm into everybody. 'Early, I expect?'

'Midday,' I said.

'That early?'

I nodded. My mum looked at us.

'They're taking no chances,' he said, my bouncing dad. 'They'll get you down there with, what, six hours to go?'

My mum was still looking at me.

'They're going to do my hair, my nails, everything,' I said. 'And my make-up.'

'Will we recognise you?' my mum said.

My dad laughed. 'She's gonna look great,' he said. 'Just imagine, my little girl on the stage at the Variety. Eh? My little Amy Peppercorn. A star. Eh?'

The telephone started ringing. My dad bounced out of his chair on the instant of the first ring. 'That'll be the phone,' he said.

My mum and I sat in what would have been silence if not for the early Saturday television.

'It's for you,' my dad bounced back in and said. 'First call of the morning. Here we go,' he said, rubbing his hands together.

I went into the hall, picked up the telephone receiver. 'Hello?'

'Amy,' a girl's voice said.

I didn't recognise the voice. 'Who's calling?'

'Amy,' she said, 'it's me, Beccs.'

I could still barely recognise her voice, it sounded so unlike her. 'Beccs?' I said. 'Surely you mean Becky?'

'Amy,' she said, seriously, 'listen. Listen. – Oh no,' she said, breaking down.

'Beccs,' I said, 'are you crying? Beccs, what's wrong?'

'Haven't you –' she stammered, 'haven't you heard? Haven't you heard what's happened?'

'Beccs,' I said, 'what's the matter?'

'Oh God!' she was crying, deeply, desperately. 'I can't believe it.'

'What?' I cried. 'Tell me what's happened.'

'It's so terrible,' she wept. 'It's terrible!'

'Beccs,' I said, trying to calm her, 'listen, you have to tell me. What's the matter? What's happened?'

'Amy!' she almost screamed. 'He's dead! He's really dead! He's *dead*!'

I glanced into the living room at the TV screen into which my parents were both still staring. 'Tell me,' I said, sickened, but somehow still calm. The telephone line went silent for a long, long time. 'Beccs?' I said. 'Beccs? Are you still there?'

There was another long, unsteady pause. I could hear Beccs breathing, breaking down, breathing again, trying to speak. 'Beccs?'

'You don't know, do you?' she said. She was crying. 'Listen,' she cried, 'listen. There was a crash – a horrible car crash, here, last night. There was some sort of stolen car. Ben was driving and –'

'Oh, my God!'

'He was being chased, by the police – in the town. They chased them – and – and – there was a crash – and – and –'

'Oh God!' I said. 'Oh God, Ben. I knew it! I just knew it! Ben!'

'No,' Beccs said, as my dad appeared at the living room door, 'no. It isn't Ben. He's – he's just in hospital. It's not Ben –' she said, breaking down. 'It's not Ben. It's Geoff. He's – Geoff's dead, Amy. It's Geoff. He's been killed. It's Geoff, Amy. Geoff's dead.'

***Car Crime

I was going to scream, really; I was.

My dad took the phone from me. He thought I was going to have another fit, I suppose, standing, as I was, struggling to breathe. A decent breath I needed, a screaming breath to tell them all this should not have happened. It shouldn't have happened, shouldn't have been happening all round me, with the telephone disappearing from my side and my parents showing so much concern. So much concern for me, it seemed too totally unrelated to Geoff and his – oh, Geoff; so tall and incongruous, so shy and stuttering and made more shy by his stutter. Geoff: curling and cringing as his mum embarrassed him so thoroughly in front of us. Geoff – Geoff!

'What's the matter?' my dad said.

My mum hovered in the background, the TV set further still in the background, still showing an aggressive ad with the spurious excitement of turbo power and the manoeuvrability of four-wheel drive.

I was going to scream, really I was. Asking me what the matter was – *asking me*! 'What's the matter?' – with my mother showing concern but my father overly worried that for some new reason the Starlight Charity Showcase would not now happen for me. He wanted it, more now than I did. He loved what was happening to his family, to himself, to me.

But what was happening to me was Car Crime; terrible, avoidable accidents that damaged and took lives and left me waiting to scream but gagging for the breath with which to achieve it. Left me! Left Geoff's mum with – with what? Car Crime? Her only child, her son a victim of the car criminals, the adrenalin junkies like Ben, compensating for their deficiencies and disappointments by attracting danger and degradation.

I was – I *was* going to scream; but what would come after? There's always a time existing after a scream. After my scream there's always a time like this, this time with my worried father taking the telephone from me and my mother showing concern in the background, saying: 'What's the matter?' for the sake of my mathematics and physics, for the Starlight Showcase, my career, my future, their own peace of mind.

They ran me a bath I didn't feel wet in, brewed me tea like hot spiky water on my tongue. My parents wanted me to feel good for something other than the death of poor Geoffrey; of which they knew nothing, as I could neither breathe properly to scream, nor speak of what was the matter with me.

Everything that had happened, all the car crimes, the driven music and the musical parasites had fashioned events through time to bring Geoffrey to his death in the passenger seat of Ben's stolen car. Ben may or may not have stolen the thing in the first place; he may or may not be responsible for killing him; but the same went for me. I may or may not be responsible for what had happened. Denying anything, eventually being forgiven was not forgetting how I was going to feel from this moment on, for the rest of my life. But at least I had a life through which to feel. Whatever I felt, I'd be here to feel it. Geoffrey wouldn't. He was done with feeling. Feeling had done with him. There was nothing left but how I felt about him, the way I felt about the things I'd put him through, the way in which I'd managed to get people to treat him. That's all there was of Geoffrey, now.

That, and his mother and his father. The rest of their lives, without him. Without him. Without him. On and on. For good. For ever. The things he would never now do. What were they? For his parents, for his mum and dad, the things he would never do were everything. There would be nothing left now, for them, but the things Geoffrey would never do.

I didn't know how badly hurt Ben was. Nobody knew. I didn't know how badly hurt I was, or Beccs. Or Kirsten. How badly hurt could we be? There was no telling. Not in this time, the time of silent screaming in my house, with my twin sisters stowed away and my parents' voices subdued for the sake of my well being. I couldn't disturb the anti-scream silence of my parents' concern with news of what had happened. It wouldn't have felt right to bring it out for their inspection, for their translation into their personal concerns for their daughter's safety and her ability to perform in front of the television cameras. I couldn't have stood for Geoffrey's poor going to have been tainted by questions about my own part in it, the circumstances that drop me here in a fit in one minute, that collect Geoff and kill him the next.

The telephone kept ringing, alarming the already shocked and dazed air clogged about my ears. I was going to scream, but the phone alarmed me again and again with calls from the local newspapers, from family and friends of my family. They called with best wishes, for requests for information; but not about Geoffrey Fryer or Ben Lyons: about me, when all I was doing I was doing with the life I had left to lead, a life amongst many in a world that abused chronically shy and stuttering people, that excluded dead people like Geoffrey Fryer. They called to wish me luck: me, the luckiest person alive – the luckiest to be alive.

But now being alive meant living this saddening shock, this selfish and horrendous regret for not having shown Geoffrey Fryer just how perfectly priceless he was. I saw him cringing with embarrassment as his mother – as she gushed in her own shyness over our names. Geoff's discomfort compared to this? Compare his fear of the grunge bullies at school to what his friends could do to him? He'd have been better off with Peter Stevens on his back, harmlessly slapping his ears. What was a bit of humiliation, compared to not being here to be humiliated at all?

Nothing. All, nothing. Geoffrey – Geoffrey Fryer, nothing. How could his poor mother ever come to terms with that? What did you do, how did you ever begin to get over it?

I let the telephone ring. I was alarmed, but several steps dislocated from the whistles and the bells of the well-wishers and my hundreds of brand new friends and admirers. My sisters shrieked down the telephone line for minutes on end, a more honest to goodness cry than the dazed silence that had overtaken my own.

My sisters cried. Beccs had cried. I was going to scream, really I was; but nothing came out. Nothing could come out of me, shored-up and stoppered as I was, somewhere several steps removed from the way I think I felt and the things I really wanted to do. I did nothing but lie in the bath without consciously getting wet, unconsciously patting dry the unconscious wet.

Dressed, neither my father's concern nor my mother's distant worry came near enough to touch me. They came to the door to see me off in the car Solar Records had sent for me, waving me away, looking forward to this evening, convinced that my face was being straightened and lengthened by nerves alone. There was nothing, everybody supposed, that could be wrong with me.

I had a dressing room of sorts, in which I sat, out of sorts, while the hairdresser bushed and made scruffy my short straight hair. There were people, performers, singers, dancers, half-dressed and laughing, talking about the show, about their past experiences and their hopes for the future. We were in a London theatre. The Variety. People on these London streets were busy about their business, shopping, eating, drinking, living; while all around me the performers busied themselves, concerned only with their own appearance and the possible effects on their performance of an extra bit of make-up here or the cut and sweep of their heavily gelled hair.

I was going to scream, really I was; but I watched my face being made-over in the dressing room mirror, watching my tearless eyes, my screamless mouth being lined and painted, tearlessly scribed and lineated, painted over, exaggerated. As Ray Ray came and went, ranted and crowed and ranted, came and went and came back again, my silence let it all go by as if it was nothing. Nothing.

'Opportunity!' Raymond Raymond, A and R man, Solar Records, ranted. 'It knocks, yeah? But rarely, know what I mean? Know what I mean?'

I knew what he meant. It all meant nothing at all. I let it all go by, as the whole afternoon went by into the early evening and the start of the show that must go on. I looked into the mirror in my dance outfit at my scruffy hair and painted face as the stage-fright nervousness of the other performers strengthened around me, and all I could feel was – was the nothing that it all was. No, I could feel Geoff, Geoffrey Fryer, the nothing that he now was. I could feel for Geoffrey Fryer's mother, but I could feel Geoff.

I was going to scream, really I was.

The compère-comedian did his bit, telling a few stand-up jokes, introducing a few acts. As I was way down the list, a little-known pop singer in the style of Ms Courtney Schaeffer, I'd soon be joked about then introduced. I was going to be a kind of little taster of the main meal to come, when Courtney would take the stage and the audience, as always, by storm. I was way down the appearance list, while Courtney was as way up the top as it was possible to be.

I waited in the wings in my make-up and costume. The Solar dancers were limbering up round me, buzzing with nerves. They knew the television cameras were out there. They could sense, could feel, could *taste* the audience on the other side of the curtain and the cameras. This was our big break. They glanced at me, with little smiles that flitted away at the sight of my dead straight face.

My straight face, for the dead. That's how I felt. No excitement. No nerves. Just a massive black hole where my racing heart should have been.

I couldn't remember the words to my song. I couldn't even remember the title of it. It didn't seem important. It didn't seem real. None of this did. I felt too flat, too two-dimensional, with the greater part of me, with the depth, missing.

There were acrobats on the stage. They were all in white, flitting and flying, brilliant in their timing and strength; but they surprised no one, not now. All the acrobatics that human beings could do had been done, again and again. Now we wanted them to fly and to fight in the air like martial arts film stars brought to real life. But all they could do was

183

fall, only to be caught in the nick of time by their caring colleagues. The audience did not care.

They wouldn't care about me, either. I could feel the tiredness of the applause as the acrobats flew from the stage; I was just another tired act going through the motions, all washed out before I'd begun to sing a single note, to take a solitary step towards the stage.

The curtain came down as the acrobats filed past us, their ordinary bodies stepping heavy on the boards of the stage. They came off as the comedian-compère told another joke; we filed on behind the curtain, positioning ourselves in the forever V, like migrating birds. The lights were down. We waited in darkness. The compère got to another punch line, the audience responded with laughter on cue as if they were contracted to laugh on time. The dancers just behind me were breathing heavily, hyperventilating with anticipation. This was it. The compère started into our introduction. We had rehearsed this again and again. We knew what was coming.

'A new singing sensation,' the compère or comedian was saying, 'I'm sure you'll want to give a warm welcome to Little Amy Peppercorn!'

The huge curtains swept back and the spotlights came on. The music started as we looked out into the massive auditorium and saw nothing. Nothing. Exactly that. All was darkness out there.

The dancers just behind me started dancing. I was supposed to be with them, a few steps, just a few, just before I'd start singing.

I looked out into the theatre against the flow of the spotlights. Nothing moved. Within me, nothing moved. The dancers stalled behind me as I stayed rooted to the spot-lit centre of the stage. Nothing moved within or without me.

The music ground to a halt. I could hear, through the new and massive silence, a confusion of voices stages left and right. I could hear Ray Ray's staccato swearing.

I stood there, looking out, looking out. The television cameras would be on me, I knew, but I couldn't feel a thing for the blankness of an uncaring audience.

This was all wrong. The houselights sensed it, coming back on, showing the rows of audience faces in tiers disappearing way up into the roof. The television cameras blinked with red LEDs from the balconies.

There was a massive, shuffling silence as the audience looked at me and I gazed back at them. I didn't know what I was doing. Everything had slipped away from inside me. I could feel myself breathing, could feel my moist eyes blinking in the houselights of the eerily silent theatre. I felt, for a moment, all the silent homes as people viewing stopped talking in their seats, stopped stirring cups of tea, to look at everything that was going wrong.

I looked to my left and to my right, up at the private boxes all lined with blank faces. I looked back out towards the faces all turned silently towards me. I looked at them all, a long, long time.

I was going to scream, really I was.

I was going to. I could already feel the spine-tingle of my scream in the roof-rafters of the theatre. My scream was going to say everything, to bring the dead ever so slightly back to life.

But the dead don't do that. No scream was ever going to be long or loud enough. Not even mine.

I was going to scream; but my mouth opened and the words came out so simply, so seemingly of their own accord:

You would seize the day for me,
  Keep the night away for me.

So simply out, simply stopped. I took a breath. It was as if I was by myself here, totally alone in front of all these faces, these pale discs with nothing written on them. The lonely, vacant spaces all round me wanted filling with my voice, with my every emotion. My voice, my every emotion flooded from me with the next line:

Make the darkness light for me,
  The noble sun ignite for me,
  If ever, if ever you were here.

My voice flew, soared, raged for my friend, Geoffrey Fryer: For Geoff:

And if ever you were here again
  I'd never shed a tear again
  Or make the sunrise mine alone
  Or see a new sun shine alone
  If ever, if ever you were here.

My voice stayed flying, flying enraged in the upper tiers of the floating theatre, floating on my voice, my every terrible emotion.

As the lights were going down, leaving a single spotlight on me, I found myself crying. Crying and crying, for Geoff:

But nothing is forever now I know
  The sunrise and the day will go.

From somewhere, from nowhere, a single, lonely violin started to play, to weave plaintively between the ebbs and flows of my voice. The words came automatically, the tears, the flooding tears too. For Geoff:

As the sun will burn to death one day
To be with you where you have gone
Where suns and stars have never shone.

I cried. I breathed and wept, for Geoff.

The orchestra, somewhere in the darkness below, joined with the lone violin, swelling the orchestral sound, flooding the auditorium with emotion. For Geoff:

Oh, you would seize the day for me
Keep fearful night away for me
Make the darkness light for me
The noble sun ignite for me.

With orchestra and voice augmenting in power, in power of emotion. For you, Geoff:

If ever,
If ever you were here with me
Once more.
Just one more day to keep
As darkness makes its way to sleep
To know that you've been near again
I'd never, ever shed a t –

With voice breaking, shattering into little pieces. My voice failed. I wept for Geoff, standing there in the spotlight with the orchestra going round the melody once again, waiting for me to regain myself. I did it. I did it for Geoff:

If ever,
If ever you were here with me (pause)
Once more
Just one more day to keep
As darkness makes its way to sleep (pause)
(Breathe, pause, breathe)

To know that you've been near again
I'd never, ever shed – a tear again!

I shed a tear. To Geoff. The song ended. I wept. Nothing happened. The spotlight remained. There was darkness, huge impossible silence.

The lights started to come up. I looked up, the tears sparkling on my face.

I looked up as the lights came up. For a moment, for a long moment, I actually believed that everyone in the audience had got up and gone home as I sang for Geoff. I looked up; the houselights showed me faces, hundreds and hundreds of faces, all concentrating on me. I wiped away a tear.

As if my gesture to wipe the tear had been a signal, the eruption happened. An explosion of calling voices and applause ripped by me, crashing through the curtains closing behind me. People were standing up. They were clapping, wildly, waving, shouting.

I had sung for Geoff. I didn't understand for the moment what they wanted from me. They shouted, they clapped. Geoff was dead. I was confused by the approval of an excited audience.

I looked to the side of the stage. Everybody was waving. Ray Ray was jumping up and down. I looked back at the audience. They were screaming.

I was going to scream, really I was. I was going to scream: I ran away.

I ran crying into the dressing room. There were a few other performers there, applying make-up, smoking, looking up in surprise as I crashed through the door and threw myself into

188

one of the chairs in front of the mirror, my head down. These few odd people didn't know anything of what I'd done. They were looking up, surprised, as I crashed in, closely followed by the dancers following me from the wings of the stage. The dancers wanted to know what I was playing at. They wanted to know who the hell I thought I was, denying them their big chance to appear on TV.

They melted away into corners out of sight as A and R Ray, the ray of black Solar light, came crashing after me. 'Back!' he bellowed at me. 'Now! Come on!'

He hoisted me from my chair before I could say anything, frogmarching me back along the chalky corridors to the wings of the stage. All the way up his few words were puffing in a wild enthusiastic temper. 'No! I thought, No! What's happening? I don't! I don't believe it! I don't believe it!' he declared, hanging me by my collar in the stage wings as the comedian-compère tried to bring the house back down to some kind of order.

The compère glanced at us, then frantically waved me onto the stage. Ray Ray bellowed in my ear. 'Fantastic! Bloody fantastic! We've arrived, kid! Go! On! Go!'

He shoved me forward as the compère collected me, holding me by the arm. The audience out the front were all still standing. 'Ladies and gentlemen!' the compère shouted into his mike. 'I give you, the new star: I give you, Little Amy Peppercorn!'

Little Amy Peppercorn. I'll never get rid of that 'little' now, because I'll never be big. Not physically, anyway. I'll be big if Ray Ray gets his way. He's been stomping round since the show, shouting down the phone-lines, arranging everything; interviews, personal appearances, copies of my show performance on video, the inclusion of that 'Little' on my current vid. Ray's going big. Ray's going interplanetary. He's going Solar, Universal – but me? I'm not so sure.

I did what I did for Geoff, not for myself. For once, not for myself. It wasn't meant for me, any of it. Geoff, I wanted to give it to you. I thought I was giving it all up, blowing it all away. I thought I was screaming.

I was going to scream, really I was; but I sang for Geoff: *The sun will burn to death one day, to be with you where you have gone*.

But Geoff's death wasn't of that kind; he had to do the absolute thing; a real dying, not the songster's version. You had to give him that. You had to, because he had it, and there is nothing anybody could or can ever do to change it. I couldn't change it; but I could change what I did and why – which was what I was trying to do. I wasn't trying to give Ray Ray something to crow about. I wasn't giving my parents leave to make up their differences and appear wet-eyed backstage to congratulate me, almost falling at my feet. But that's what they did. What I did was being taken from me, used to further Ray Ray's career, used to repair my parents' ailing marriage, used to create an effect that should have spoiled an event, not made one.

The newspapers were on to me. I was front page of the small papers, page four or five of the broadsheets. Whatever size the paper, I was in it, on it, part of it, news. Hot property, me; with pictures of my tears in close up, pictures of me wiping tears from my face, pictures of members of the audience, all in tears. The papers were awash with tears without one single mention of Geoffrey Fryer or his mother or father, or of their pain, or mine.

I was carried from the theatre in a daze of false publicity and speechless misunderstanding. There was nothing I could do to persuade everyone – *everyone*, that they'd got it all wrong. Even my mum smiled and blinked and smiled again, purely because she hadn't yet seen the report on the car crash that had yet to be written in the local paper that was yet to be published. The truth would come out, however locally, eventually. The details of Geoff's death and Ben's injuries would be public knowledge, but too late. I'll have been carried away on this wave of wild controversy into a celebrity paradise, a good fortune based on nothing but falsehood and untold truths.

Maybe that's the way it is, up there, in the never-never, headless world of celebrity? It is based on a face in the newspapers wiping away a misunderstood tear, the right emotion wrongly appreciated. I felt fake. I felt stupid. I collected adoration like worthless money.

'This translates!' Ray Ray bellowed into my father's face. 'Mega-bucks!'

My dad looked tipsily flushed towards my mother as she blinked and smiled and forgot she was now as ordinary a teacher as any class instructor I'd ever suffered by.

Cameras flashed in my face. All the way home I couldn't see anything but the harmful flickering of the image-capturing press and public. All night I saw them, flashing on and off in a near-epileptic fervour.

All night, far away into the next day, yet still I do not know what has actually happened. I know what everybody thinks has happened, as the press snap happy in our front garden, with my father genially holding them off while my mother entertains. She entertains the stream of consciousness that constitutes the line or queue of well-wishers appearing out of curiosity to gaze and to clap-trap over the sincerity of my last-night's performance. Ray Ray is entertained, again and again, as he barks down the telephone lines, disappears, returns, is entertained. Is revered. Ray make it happen, it happen. Big time.

Big time happening spin me into whirl of confusion and unhappiness. I don't know what has happened, big time. I can't even think about Ben without my head spinning. All I can think of is Beccs, of Becky, of Rebecca; all of them, she is. I have to see her. There's nobody else I can turn to.

The house is full of whirl and queue and clap-trap. The house entertains. I have to go to the bathroom, lock myself away for a while. None of this makes sense now. I have to make sense of something.

So I slide from bathroom to bedroom, cloak myself in long coat and winter hat, too warm for this weather. At the back of our house, it's possible to get through the hedge into the garden of the house behind. In frock coat and fur hat I go in early summer, breezing past Mr Wilson, who lives there, in his garden staring at me passing. I coolly go, thinking nothing but the sense of sense I must get. I'm going to it. I am running to it.

Somewhere along the way, I lose my hat. Perhaps on purpose, I don't know; but Beccs, Becky, Rebecca doesn't notice anything but my face when her mother shows me standing in a long coat on their front doorstep.

We stare at each other for a moment, a long moment, if there can be such a thing. Another moment, another passes before Beccs steps out of the house and clasps me to her. I hold on to her. We hold each other, free falling, our tears, what it all means.

'What does it all mean?' I ask her.

'I don't know,' she whispers. 'Something, though. It has to mean something, doesn't it?'

Beccs doesn't know how badly hurt Ben is. We are waiting to hear. She doesn't know how badly hurt we are. Or Kirsten. 'We watched you last night,' she tells me, 'on TV. My mum and I. We watched what happened.'

'They –' I say, stumbling, 'they – they didn't understand.'

'I know,' she says.

We are drinking tea. Her house entertains only me. Her mother has left us alone to talk. Becca's mother knows far more than mine. She understands to leave us alone.

'I know,' Beccs says. She smiles at me. I can't smile yet. 'You did it for Geoff, didn't you?'

I nod. A tear falls from one of us. I'm not sure which, but it belongs to us both. We can both feel it.

'Becky,' I say, 'I –'

'Beccs,' she says, quietly but quickly. 'I'm Beccs. Kirsten calls me Becky, that's fine. You call me Beccs, that's fine too.'

193

A tear falls, shared. I can hardly speak.

'Kirsty called me,' Beccs says, 'this morning. She wanted to know if I'd watched what you did last night.'

'Did she?'

'She wanted to know if I'd seen the papers this morning.'

'And have you?'

Beccs nods. 'Yes,' she says. 'Kirsty wanted to get me to agree with her. She wanted me to say it was a cheap trick and you're only out for one thing. She wanted me to say that you're a nasty little opportunist using everybody for your own publicity.'

There were suddenly no tears; but I could still hardly breathe. Beccs and I were looking, closely, into each other's eyes.

'She's jealous of you,' Beccs eventually said. 'Well, we all are, but Kirsty is especially. I wouldn't give her what she wanted. I know you. I saw what you did. It was a lovely thing, and only you and I really understand it.'

'Beccs –' I say. 'It – I –'

'And do you know what you've got to do now?' she says.

I shake my head. I love her.

She goes over to the table, comes back with one of the smaller dailies with my tearful image plastered over the front page. 'Have you seen this?' she says.

I nod. 'Yes, I've –'

'No,' she says, 'not that: this!' – as she turns to the features pages much further in. 'Look at this.'

As she spreads the news-sheet between us, I can see a picture of Courtney Schaeffer with a particularly sour expression on her face.

'Listen to this,' Beccs says, reading from the page. 'Courtney remains totally unimpressed by the reception given to newcomer, Little Amy Peppercorn, who has stolen the show

194

from under the star's nose. "My mother quite liked what she did," Courtney was reported as saying after the show. "I suppose it was all right, if you like that sort of thing." '

Beccs looks up at me. She smiles. I try a smile. It nearly fits.

'We can't let her get away with that,' Beccs says.

'Can't we?'

' "My mother quite liked what she did?" Well, my mother quite liked what Courtney did, but I didn't care for it. In fact, I hated it. You were a million times better. You've got a better voice.'

'Beccs, I –'

'No, Amy, listen. You've got to show her what we're made of.'

Now I can smile. Now it fits.

'You've got the better voice, Amy. You can do it. You've got to show her, right?'

'Have I?'

'Yes. You've got to. You've absolutely got to. She's asking for it, right?'

We're smiling at each other, about to laugh.

'Right?' Beccs says. 'Amy? Right? You've got to show her what we're made of, right? Right?'

Right.

the first chapter from the second book about
Amy Peppercorn

I've never told anyone this before, but I'll tell you: I'd have hated not to go on with it. If Beccs hadn't wanted me to continue, I would have given it all up, the singing, the money, the fame, everything; but I know I'd have always wanted to find out what would have happened. Well, I have found out, because Beccs wanted me to do it. So I can tell you.

Beccs was still my best friend. Without that, without her, I don't think I could have gone through with it. Hers was the only opinion I cared about, at the time. Even my mother seemed to abandon her principles in the excitement and hysteria of what was happening to me. My dad was mad for it, right from the start. Raymond Raymond, principal A and R man at Solar Records, and now my manager with a five-year contract that seems to have control over everything I do and say and think and feel – well, what could you expect of Ray Ray? 'Got to be!' he'd rattle out like a machine gun going off accidentally. 'Got to be! Right for it! Dead right for it!'

'Dead right for it,' my dad incanted, happily up to his elbows in the drama of our kitchen sink, with my twin baby sisters, Georgie and Jo, suspended from his braces.

'I hope you're right,' my mum worried, but soon shuffled off caution with the excitement of her eldest daughter's tearful face on the front pages of the kind of papers she had always despised. 'You are right,' she too recited, falling in line with my dad and my manager, the orchestrator of my very life. Even my meticulous and intelligent mum couldn't resist Ray Ray's most concentrated laser light.

'Got to be! Right for it! Dead right for it!'

But I didn't feel right for it. I felt like a fraud. I felt like everything Kirsty McCloud thought of me. If my best friend Beccs Bradley hadn't told me it was all right, then it wouldn't have been all right.

Even then, it wasn't, entirely. 'We have to give Courtney Schaeffer a run for her money,' Beccs said, which was a good enough reason not to throw the whole thing away, but it wasn't enough to make it all all right. It wasn't enough to make me anything other than riding high on wrongly wrought emotions, on the back of Geoff Fryer's death and everything that went with it.

I went with it because Beccs said so and I didn't have it in me to decide anything for myself. Beccs was just as hurt, just as traumatised as me; but she always had a way of focusing on things. I didn't have anything in me but Geoff's dying and Ben Lyons's remand as soon as he got out of hospital. Geoffrey Fryer was gone, entirely; and so, it seemed, was Ben. Beccs and I cried in each other's arms. The papers were full of wrong tears. My mum and dad had lost their minds in Ray Ray's gun-stuttering enthusiastic utterances. Geoffrey Fryer wasn't there. I couldn't get through to Ben's mobile. He'd be switched off, perhaps entirely, not yet really under-standing what had happened, what he'd done. And what he'd done, he'd done to us all, a car crime that crashed into and affected or ruined so many, many lives.

But Beccs said I should do it, that I should show the world what we were made of. We were, I was feeling, made of completely the wrong stuff to show the world anything. My point of view was swerving from one extreme to the other, with every tick of Becca's mum's living room clock. One second I was an innocent party, a bystander caught up in uncontrollable events, the next I felt as guilty as a murderer. My unwarranted but impending stardom swayed with me, adding to the weight of the clock-pendulum, swinging me from elated and nervous happiness to massive, overbearing guilt as Beccs's tears ticked with my own into the future of what we would or would not show the world.

'What does it all mean?' I asked Beccs.

'I don't know,' she whispered. 'Something, though. It has to mean something, doesn't it?'

Everything had to mean something, didn't it? Or what was the point of anything? Beccs decided that the point was that I had intended to do something, to say something for Geoff. For you, Geoff. Beccs knew; she understood my motives, my reasons, despite what her cousin Kirsty would have her believe. Beccs allowed me to believe in a meaning, a reason and a purpose. We cried together, looking for and finding our purpose.

It was Beccs, my best friend, I had to thank, or blame, for my walk back through the warm streets with her to my house where the press and my parents waited frantically for me with a frantic Ray Ray stuttering admonitions and obscenities in a vicious spray of invective.

'She better not. Again. It doesn't do. Not now. We need control. You know? You know? Control? Control!' he freaked.

My mum looked at Becca's hand in mine, noting, above everyone, how hard we held on to one another. My mum, I thought for a moment, was showing the kind of concern that understood my anguish, my friend's anguish, our shared handhold mutually reaching for something more solid than all this fury of raised voice and frantic ambition. She looked at us, my mum, only until Ray Ray's greater insistence took her attention, holding it at least as tightly as I was holding Beccs's hand and she mine.

'It's gotta be control, yeah?' Ray blasted. 'Without it, nothing. With, all! Yeah? All! Everything to play for! These are big stakes. Big breaks, though. The best. The best ever. This is it. All it needs, control, yeah?'

'Yeah,' my dad said. He was being sent to collect the twins from his sister's, where they'd spent my big night last night. The press wanted the Peppercorns completely; so my dad would gather them from wherever for the family photos.

My mum was glowing with pride on a telephone red-hot from continually ringing, from continually being answered. She had to shout to be heard above Raymond Raymond barking like a guard dog at everything that threatened me or promised us success.

Nobody said anything to Beccs. Nobody said a word to her, including me. I was trying to hold on to her, trying, failing. Too many telephone calls, too many photo opportunities, too many other, very interested people turning up at our little house for their own or everybody else's self-interested reasons. Beccs looked at me from the other side of the room as I was positioned in a better light, or poised shaking hands with one after another self-interested party. She looked at me across the turmoil of my success smiling simply, encouragingly; but she looked, from where I was being led, as if she was smiling from one place into another; from one, into an entirely separated, untouchable place. She nodded at me across the distance rapidly expanding between us, as if to tell me to go on, even without her. I didn't want to go without her, but she nodded to me to continue.

I can't tell you what that was like. I had to carry on. I *did* carry on, as you know, because so much has happened. Some

of it you might have read about. You might have even been
to see me in that time; I wonder if you have? I hope you have,
then when I tell you what it was like, you might begin to feel
you've been there with me, at least for part of the way.